Inspector Bucket's Job

Charles Dickens

Fredonia Books
Amsterdam, The Netherlands

Inspector Bucket's Job

by
Charles Dickens

ISBN: 1-4101-0770-1

Fredonia Books
Amsterdam, The Netherlands
http://www.fredoniabooks.com

Charles Dickens

Inspector Bucket's Job

One of the most natural of story-tellers, and also one who took most naturally to the "detective" or "mystery" form was Charles Dickens. His lovers can easily recall examples, not only in the so-called detective stories such as "The Mystery of Edwin Drood," but in the shape of exciting threads that wind through and color some of his broadest efforts, such as "Little Dorrit."

One of Dickens' great admirations was Inspector Field, a London detective. He reported him in a series of articles, describing his own adventures in the slums with police guards. He saw in him the good-natured, native shrewdness, the kindliness towards the distressed, yet the inflexibility of vengeance itself with the criminal, that one would expect from the tender-hearted author himself were he to turn detective.

With such "Real Life" to work from, no wonder Dickens put one of the best detective stories of all time into his lengthy novel of "Bleak House," from which it has been selected for the following pages. The "Inspector Bucket" of this story is none other than Inspector Field, and the episode in Chapter VIII is a vivid and literal rendering of Dickens' own visits to the dreadful depths of the London slums with his friend of the police.

Charles Dickens

Inspector Bucket's Job

I

IN FASHION

VOLUMNIA, LADY DEDLOCK has returned to her house in town for a few days previous to her departure for Paris, where her ladyship intends to stay some weeks; after which her movements are uncertain. The fashionable intelligence says so, for the comfort of the Parisians, and it knows all fashionable things. To know things otherwise, were to be unfashionable. My Lady Dedlock has been down at what she calls, in familiar conversation, her "place" in Lincolnshire. The waters are out in Lincolnshire. An arch of the bridge in the park has been sapped and sopped away. The adjacent low-lying ground, for half a mile in breadth, is a stagnant river, with melancholy trees for islands in it, and a surface punctured all over, all day long, with falling rain. My Lady Dedlock's "place" has been extremely dreary. The weather, for many a day and night, has been so wet that the trees seem wet through, and the soft loppings and prunings of the woodman's ax can make no crash or crackle as they fall. The deer, looking soaked, leave quagmires, where they pass. The shot of a rifle loses its sharpness in the moist air, and its smoke moves in a tardy little cloud towards the green rise, coppice-topped, that makes a background for the falling rain. The view from my Lady Dedlock's own windows is alternately a lead-colored view, and a view in Indian ink. The vases on the stone terrace in the foreground catch the rain all day; and the heavy drops fall, drip, drip, drip, upon the broad flagged pavement, called, from old time, the Ghost's Walk, all night. On Sundays, the little church in the park is moldy; the oaken pulpit breaks out into a cold sweat; and there is a general smell and taste as of the ancient Dedlocks in their graves. My Lady Dedlock (who is childless), looking out in the early twilight from her boudoir at a keeper's lodge, and seeing the light of a fire upon the latticed panes, and smoke rising from the chimney, and a child, chased by a woman, running out into the rain to meet the shining figure of a wrapped-up man coming through the gate, has been put quite out of temper. My Lady Dedlock says she has been "bored to death."

Therefore my Lady Dedlock has come away from the place in Lincolnshire, and has left it to the rain, and the crows, and the rabbits, and the deer, and the partridges and pheasants. The pictures of the Dedlocks past and gone have seemed to vanish into the damp walls in mere lowness of spirits, as the housekeeper has passed along the old rooms, shutting up the shutters. And when they will next come forth again, the fashionable intelligence—which, like the fiend, is omniscient of the past and present, but not the future—cannot yet undertake to say.

Sir Leicester Dedlock is only a baronet, but there is no mightier baronet than he. His family is as old as the hills, and infinitely more respectable. He has a general opinion that the world might get on without hills, but would be done up without Dedlocks. He would on the whole admit Nature to be a good idea (a little low, perhaps, when not inclosed with a park-fence), but an idea dependent for its execution on your great country families. He is a gentleman of strict conscience, disdainful of all littleness and meanness, and ready, on the shortest notice, to die any death you may please to mention rather than give occasion for the least impeachment of his integrity. He is an honorable, obstinate, truthful, high-spirited, intensely prejudiced, perfectly unreasonable man.

Sir Leicester is twenty years, full measure, older than

my Lady. He will never see sixty-five again, nor perhaps sixty-six, nor yet sixty-seven. He has a twist of the gout now and then, and walks a little stiffly. He is of a worthy present, with his light gray hair and whiskers, his fine shirt-frill, his pure white waistcoat, and his blue coat with bright buttons always buttoned. He is ceremonious, stately, most polite on every occasion to my Lady, and holds her personal attractions in the highest estimation. His gallantry to my Lady, which has never changed since he courted her, is the one little touch of romantic fancy in him.

Indeed, he married her for love. A whisper still goes about, that she had not even family; howbeit, Sir Leicester had so much family that perhaps he had enough, and could dispense with any more. But she had beauty, pride, ambition, insolent resolve, and sense enough to portion out a legion of fine ladies. Wealth and station, added to these, soon floated her upward; and for years, now, my Lady Dedlock has been at the center of the fashionable intelligence, and at the top of the fashionable tree.

How Alexander wept when he had no more worlds to conquer, everybody knows—or has some reason to know by this time, the matter having been rather frequently mentioned. My Lady Dedlock, having conquered *her* world, fell, not into the melting, but rather into the freezing mood. An exhausted composure, a worn-out placidity, an equanimity of fatigue not to be ruffled by interest or satisfaction, are the trophies of her victory. She is perfectly well-bred. If she could be translated to Heaven to-morrow, she might be expected to ascend without any rapture.

She has beauty still, and if it be not in its heyday, it is not yet in its autumn. She has a fine face—originally of a character that would be rather called very pretty than handsome, but improved into classicality by the acquired expression of her fashionable state. Her figure is elegant, and has the effect of being tall. Not that she is so, but that "the most is made," as the Honorable Bob Stables has frequently asserted upon oath, "of all her points." The same authority observes, that she is perfectly got up;

and remarks, in commendation of her hair especially, that she is the best-groomed woman in the whole stud.

With all her perfections on her head, my Lady Dedlock has come up from her place in Lincolnshire (hotly pursued by the fashionable intelligence), to pass a few days at her house in town previous to her departure for Paris, where her ladyship intends to stay some weeks, after which her movements are uncertain. And at her house in town, upon this muddy, murky afternoon, presents himself an old-fashioned old gentleman, attorney-at-law, and eke solicitor of the High Court of Chancery, who has the honor of acting as legal adviser of the Dedlocks, and has as many cast-iron boxes in his office with that name outside, as if the present baronet were the coin of the conjuror's trick, and were constantly being juggled through the whole set. Across the hall, and up the stairs, and along the passages, and through the rooms, which are very brilliant in the season and very dismal out of it—Fairy-land to visit, but a desert to live in—the old gentleman is conducted, by a Mercury in powder, to my Lady's presence.

The old gentleman is rusty to look at, but is reputed to have made good thrift out of aristocratic marriage settlements and aristocratic wills, and to be very rich. He is surrounded by a mysterious halo of family confidences; of which he is known to be the silent depository. There are noble Mausoleums rooted for centuries in retired glades of parks, among the growing timber and the fern, which perhaps hold fewer noble secrets than walk abroad among men, shut up in the breast of Mr. Tulkinghorn. He is of what is called the old school—a phrase generally meaning any school that seems never to have been young—and wears knee breeches tied with ribbons, and gaiters or stockings. One peculiarity of his black clothes, and of his black stockings, be they silk or worsted, is, that they never shine. Mute, close, irresponsive to any glancing light, his dress is like himself. He never converses, when not professionally consulted. He is found sometimes, speechless but quite at home, at corners of dinner-tables in great country houses, and near doors of drawing-rooms, concerning which the fashionable intelligence is eloquent: where everybody knows him, and where half the Peerage stops to say "How do you do, Mr. Tulkinghorn?" He receives these salutations with gravity, and buries them along with the rest of his knowledge.

Sir Leicester Dedlock is with my Lady, and is happy to see Mr. Tulkinghorn. There is an air of prescription about him which is always agreeable to Sir Leicester; he receives it as a kind of tribute. He likes Mr. Tulkinghorn's dress: there is a kind of tribute in that too. It is eminently respectable, and likewise, in a general way, retainer-like. It expresses, as it were, the steward of the legal mysteries, the butler of the legal cellar, of the Dedlocks.

Has Mr. Tulkinghorn any idea of this himself? It may be so, or it may not; but there is this remarkable circumstance to be noted in everything associated with my Lady Dedlock as one of a class—as one of the leaders and representatives of her little world. She supposes herself to be an inscrutable Being, quite out of the reach and ken of ordinary mortals—seeing herself in her glass, where indeed she looks so. Yet, every dim little star revolving about her, from her maid to the manager of the Italian Opera, knows her weaknesses, prejudices, follies, haughtinesses, and caprices; and lives upon as accurate a calculation and as nice a measure of her moral nature, as her dressmaker takes of her physical proportions. Is a new dress, a new custom, a new singer, a new dancer, a new form of jewelry, a new dwarf or giant, a new chapel, a new anything, to be set up? There are deferential people, in a dozen callings, whom my Lady Dedlock suspects of nothing but prostration before her, who can tell you how to manage her as if she were a baby; who do nothing but nurse her all their lives; who, humbly affecting to follow with profound subservience, lead her and her whole troop after them; who, in hooking one, hook all and bear them off, as Lemuel Gulliver bore away the stately fleet of the majestic Lilliput. "If you want to address our people, sir," say Blaze and Sparkle

the jewellers—meaning by our people, Lady Dedlock and the rest—" you must remember that you are not dealing with the general public; you must hit our people in their weakest place, and their weakest place is such a place."
" To make this article go down, gentlemen," say Sheen and Gloss the mercers, to their friends the manufacturers, " you must come to us, because we know where to have the fashionable people, and we can make it fashionable."
" If you want to get this print upon the tables of my high connection, sir," says Mr. Sladdery the librarian, " or if you want to get this dwarf or giant into the houses of my high connection, sir, or if you want to secure to this enter- tainment, the patronage of my high connection, sir, you must leave it, if you please, to me; for I have been ac- customed to study the leaders of my high connection, sir; and I may tell you, without vanity, that I can turn them round my finger,"—in which Mr. Sladdery, who is an honest man, does not exaggerate at all.

Therefore, while Mr. Tulkinghorn may not know what is passing in the Dedlock mind at present, it is very possible that he may.

" My Lady's cause has been again before the Chancellor, has it, Mr. Tulkinghorn ? " says Sir Leicester, giving him his hand.

" Yes. It has been on again to-day," Mr. Tulkinghorn replies, making one of his quiet bows to my Lady who is on a sofa near the fire, shading her face with a hand-screen.

" It would be useless to ask," says my Lady, with the dreariness of the place in Lincolnshire still upon her, " whether anything has been done."

" Nothing that *you* would call anything, has been done to-day," replies Mr. Tulkinghorn.

" Nor ever will be," says my Lady.

Sir Leicester has no objection to an interminable Chan- cery suit. It is a slow, expensive, British, constitutional kind of thing. To be sure, he has not a vital interest in the suit in question, her part in which was the only property my Lady brought him; and he has a shadowy impression that for his name—the name of Dedlock—to be in a cause, and not in the title of that cause is a most ridiculous accident. But he regards the Court of Chancery, even if it should involve an occasional delay of justice and a trifling amount of confusion, as a something, devised in conjunction with a variety of other somethings, by the perfection of human wisdom, for the eternal settlement (humanly speaking) of everything. And he is upon the whole of a fixed opinion, that to give the sanction of his countenance to any complaints respecting it, would be to encourage some person in the lower classes to rise up somewhere—like Wat Tyler.

"As a few fresh affidavits have been put upon the file," says Mr. Tulkinghorn, "and as they are short, and as I proceed upon the troublesome principle of begging leave to posess my clients with any new proceedings in a cause;" cautious man Mr. Tulkinghorn, taking no more responsibility than necessary; "and further, as I see you are going to Paris; I have brought them in my pocket."

(Sir Leicester was going to Paris too, by-the-bye, but the delight of the fashionable intelligence was in his Lady.)

Mr. Tulkinghorn takes out his papers, asks permission to place them on a golden talisman of a table at my Lady's elbow, puts on his spectacles, and begins to read by the light of a shaded lamp.

"'In Chancery. Between John Jarndyce——'"

My Lady interrupts, requesting him to miss as many of the formal horrors as he can.

Mr. Tulkinghorn glances over his spectacles, and begins again lower down. My Lady carelessly and scornfully abstracts her attention. Sir Leicester in a great chair looks at the fire, and appears to have a stately liking for the legal repetitions and prolixities, as ranging among the national bulwarks. It happens that the fire is hot, where my Lady sits; and that the hand-screen is more beautiful than useful, being priceless but small. My Lady, changing her position, sees the papers on the table—looks at them nearer —looks at them nearer still—asks impulsively:

15

" Who copied that? "

Mr. Tulkinghorn stops short, surprised by my Lady's animation and her unusual tone.

" Is it what you people call law-hand? " she asks, looking full at him in her careless way again, and toying with her screen.

" Not quite. Probably "—Mr. Tulkinghorn examines it as he speaks—" the legal character which it has, was acquired after the original hand was formed. Why do you ask? "

" Anything to vary this detestable monotony. O, go on, do! "

Mr. Tulkinghorn reads again. The heat is greater, my Lady screens her face. Sir Leicester doses, starts up suddenly, and cries " Eh? what do you say? "

" I say I am afraid," says Mr. Tulkinghorn, who had risen hastily, " that Lady Dedlock is ill."

" Faint," my Lady murmurs, with white lips, " only that; but it is like the faintness of death. Don't speak to me. Ring, and take me to my room! "

Mr. Tulkinghorn retires into another chamber, bells ring, feet shuffle and patter, silence ensues. Mercury at last begs Mr. Tulkinghorn to return.

" Better now," quoth Sir Leicester, motioning the lawyer to sit down and read to him alone. " I have been quite alarmed. I never knew my Lady to swoon before. But the weather is extremely trying—and she really has been bored to death down at our place in Lincolnshire."

II

THE LAW-WRITER

IN the eastern borders of Chancery Lane, that is to say, more particularly in Cook's Court, Cursitor Street, Mr. Snagsby, Law-Stationer, pursues his lawful calling. In the shade of Cook's Court, at most times a shady place, Mr. Snagsby has dealt in all sorts of blank forms of legal process; in skins and rolls of parchment; in paper—foolscap, brief, draft, brown, white, whitey-brown, and blotting; in stamps; in office-quills, pens, ink, and India-rubber, pounce, pins, pencils, sealing-wax, and wafers; in red tape and green ferret; in pocket-books, almanacs, diaries, and law lists; in string boxes, rules, inkstands—glass and leaden, penknives, scissors, bodkins, and other small office-cutlery; in short, in articles too numerous to mention; ever since he was out of his time, and went into partnership with Peffer. On that occasion, Cook's Court was in a manner revolutionized by the new inscription in fresh paint, PEFFER and SNAGSBY, displacing the time-honored and not easily to be deciphered legend, PEFFER, only. For smoke, which is the London ivy, had so wreathed itself round Peffer's name, and clung to his dwelling-place, that the affectionate parasite overpowered the parent tree.

Peffer is never seen in Cook's Court now. He is not expected there, for he has been recumbent this quarter of a century in the churchyard of St. Andrew's, Holborn, with the waggons and hackney-coaches roaring past him, all the day and half the night, like one great dragon. If he ever steal forth when the dragon is at rest, to air himself again in Cook's Court, until admonished to return by the crowing of the sanguine cock in the cellar at the little dairy in Cursitor Street, whose ideas of daylight it would be curious to ascertain, since he knows from his personal observation next to nothing about it—if Peffer ever do revisit the pale glimpses of Cook's Court, which no law-stationer in the trade can positively deny, he comes invisibly, and no one is the worse or wiser.

In his lifetime, and likewise in the period of Snagsby's "time" of seven long years, there dwelt with Peffer, in the same law-stationer premises, a niece—a short, shrewd niece, something too violently compressed about the waist, and with a sharp nose like a sharp autumn evening, inclining to be frosty towards the end. The Cook's-Courtiers had a rumor flying among them, that the mother of this niece did, in her daughter's childhood, moved by too jealous a solicitude that her figure should approach perfection, lace her up every morning with her maternal foot against the bed-post for a stronger hold and purchase; and further, that she exhibited internally pints of vinegar and lemon-juice: which acids, they held, had mounted to the nose and temper of the patient. With whichsoever of the many tongues of Rumor this frothy report originated, it either never reached, or never influenced, the ears of young Snagsby; who, having wooed and won its fair subject on his arrival at man's estate, entered into two partnerships at once. So now, in Cook's Court, Cursitor Street, Mr. Snagsby and the niece are one; and the niece still cherishes her figure—which, however tastes may differ, is unquestionably so far precious, that there is mighty little of it.

Mr. and Mrs. Snagsby are not only one bone and one flesh, but, to the neighbors' thinking, one voice too. That voice, appearing to proceed from Mrs. Snagsby alone, is heard in Cook's Court very often. Mr. Snagsby, otherwise than as he finds expression, through these dulcet tones, is rarely heard. He is a mild, bald, timid man, with a shining head, and a scrubby clump of black hair sticking out at the back. He tends to meekness and obesity. As he stands at his door in Cook's Court, in his gray shop-coat and black calico sleeves, looking up at the clouds; or stands behind a desk in his dark shop, with a heavy flat ruler, snipping and slicing at sheepskin, in company with his two 'prentices; he is emphatically a retiring and unassuming man. From beneath his feet, at such times, as from a shrill ghost unquiet in its grave, there frequently arise complainings and lamentations in the voice already mentioned; and haply, on some occasions, when these reach a sharper pitch than usual, Mr. Snagsby mentions to the 'prentices, " I think my little woman is a-giving it to Guster ! "

This proper name, so used by Mr. Snagsby, has before now sharpened the wit of the Cook's-Courtiers to remark that it ought to be the name of Mrs. Snagsby; seeing that she might with great force and expression be termed a Guster, in compliment to her stormy character. It is, however, the possession, and the only possession, except fifty shillings per annum and a very small box indifferently filled with clothing, of a lean young woman from a workhouse (by some supposed to have been christened Augusta); who, although she was farmed or contracted for, during her growing time, by an amiable benefactor of his species resident at Tooting, and cannot fail to have been developed under the most favorable circumstances, " has fits "—which the parish can't account for.

Guster, really aged three or four and twenty, but looking around ten years older, goes cheap with this unaccountable drawback of fits; and is so apprehensive of being returned on the hands of her patron saint, that except when she is found with her head in the pail, or the sink, or the copper, or the dinner, or anything else that happens to be near her at the time of her seizure, she is always at work. She is a satisfaction to the parents and guardians of the 'prentices, who feel that there is little danger of her inspiring tender emotions in the breast of youth; she is a satisfaction to Mrs. Snagsby, who can always find fault with her; she is a satisfaction to Mr. Snagsby, who thinks it a charity to keep her. The law-stationer's establishment is, in Guster's eyes, a Temple of plenty and splendor. She believes the little drawing-room upstairs, always kept, as one may say, with its hair in papers and its pinafore on, to be the most elegant apartment in Christendom. The view it commands of Cook's Court at one end (not to mention a squint into Cursitor Street), and of Coavinses the sheriff's officer's backyard at the other, she regards as a prospect of unequaled beauty. The portraits it displays in oil—and plenty of it too—of Mr. Snagsby looking at Mrs. Snagsby, and of Mrs. Snagsby looking at Mr. Snagsby, are in her eyes as achievements of Raphael or Titian. Guster has some recompenses for her many privations.

Mr. Snagsby refers everything not in the practical mysteries of the business to Mrs. Snagsby. She manages the money, reproaches the tax-gatherers, appoints the times and places of devotion on Sunday, licenses Mr. Snagsby's entertainments, and acknowledges no responsibility as to what she thinks fit to provide for dinner; insomuch that she is the high standard of comparison among the neighboring wives, a long way down Chancery Lane on both sides, and even out in Holborn, who, in any domestic passages of arms, habitually call upon their husbands to look at the difference between their (the wives') position and Mrs. Snagsby's, and their (the husbands') behavior and Mr. Snagsby's. Rumor always flying, bat-like, about Cook's Court, and skimming in and out at everybody's windows, does say that Mrs. Snagsby is jealous and inquisitive; and that Mr. Snagsby is sometimes worried out of house and home, and that if he had the spirit of a mouse he wouldn't stand it. It is even observed, that the wives who quote him to their self-willed husbands as a shining example, in reality look down upon him; and that nobody does so with greater superciliousness than one particular lady, whose lord is more than suspected of laying his umbrella on her as an instrument of correction. But these vague whisperings may arise from Mr. Snagsby's being, in his way, rather a meditative and poetical man; loving to walk in Staple Inn in the summer time, and to observe how countrified the sparrows and the leaves are; also to lounge about the Rolls Yard of a Sunday afternoon, and to remark (if in good spirits) that there were old times once, and that you'd find a stone coffin or two, now, under that chapel, he'll be bound, if you was to dig for it. He solaces his imagination, too, by thinking of the many Chancellors and Vices, and Masters of the Rolls, who are deceased; and he gets such a flavor of the country out of telling the two 'prentices how he *has* heard say that a brook " as clear as crystal " once ran down the middle of Holborn, when Turnstile really was a turnstile, leading slap away into the meadows—gets such a flavor of the country out of this, that he never wants to go there.

The day is closing in and the gas is lighted, but is not yet fully effective, for it is not quite dark. Mr. Snagsby standing at his shop-door, looking up at the clouds, sees a crow, who is out late, skim westward over the slice of sky belonging to Cook's Court. The crow flies straight across Chancery Lane and Lincoln's Inn Garden, into Lincoln's Inn Fields.

Here, in a large house, formerly a house of state, lives Mr. Tulkinghorn. It is let off in sets of chambers now; and in those shrunken fragments of its greatness, lawyers lie like maggots in nuts. But its roomy staircases, passages, and antechambers still remain; and even its painted ceilings, where Allegory, in Roman helmet and celestial linen, sprawls among balustrades and pillars, flowers, clouds, and big-legged boys, and makes the head ache—as would seem to be Allegory's object always, more or less. Here, among his many boxes labeled with transcendent names, lives Mr. Tulkinghorn, when not speechlessly at home in country-houses where the great ones of the earth are bored to death. Here he is to-day, quiet at his table. An Oyster of the old school, whom nobody can open.

Like as he is to look at, so is his apartment in the dusk of the present afternoon. Rusty, out of date, withdrawing from attention, able to afford it. Heavy broad-backed, old-fashioned mahogany and horsehair chairs, not easily lifted, obsolete tables with spindle-legs and dusty baize covers, presentation prints of the holders of great titles in the last generation, or the last but one, environ him. A thick and dingy Turkey-carpet muffles the floor where he sits, attended by two candles in old-fashioned silver candlesticks, that give a very insufficient light to his large room. The titles on the backs of his books have retired into the binding; everything that can have a lock has got one; no key is visible. Very few loose papers are about. He has some manuscript near him, but is not referring to it. With the round top of an inkstand, and two broken bits of sealing-wax, he is silently and slowly working out whatever train of indecision is in his mind. Now, the inkstand top is in the middle: now, the red bit of sealing-wax, now the black bit. That's not it. Mr. Tulkinghorn must gather them all up and begin again.

Here, beneath the painted ceiling, with fore-shortened Allegory staring down at his intrusion as if it meant to swoop upon him, and he cutting it dead, Mr. Tulkinghorn has at once his house and office. He keeps no staff; only one middle-aged man, usually a little out at elbows, who sits in a high pew in the hall, and is rarely overburdened with business. Mr. Tulkinghorn is not in a common way. He wants no clerks. He is a great reservoir of confidences, not to be so tapped. His clients want *him;* he is all in all. Drafts that he requires to be drawn, are drawn by special pleaders in the Temple on mysterious instructions; fair copies that he requires to be made, are made at the stationers', expense being no consideration. The middle-aged man in the pew, knows scarcely more of the affairs of the Peerage, than any crossing-sweeper in Holborn.

The red bit, the black bit, the inkstand top, the other inkstand top, the little sand-box. So! You to the middle, you to the right, you to the left. This train of indecision must surely be worked out now or never.—Now! Mr. Tulkinghorn gets up, adjusts his spectacles, puts on his hat, puts the manuscript in his pocket, goes out, tells the middle-aged man out at elbows, " I shall be back presently." Very rarely tells him anything more explicit.

Mr. Tulkinghorn goes, as the crow came—not quite so straight, but nearly—to Cook's Court, Cursitor Street. To Snagsby's, Law Stationer's, Deeds engrossed and copied, Law-writing executed in all its branches, etc., etc., etc.

It is somewhere about five or six o'clock in the afternoon, and a balmy fragrance of warm tea hovers in Cook's Court. It hovers about Snagsby's door. The hours are early there; dinner at half-past one, and supper at half-past nine. Mr. Snagsby was about to descend into the subterranean regions to take tea, when he looked out of his door just now, and saw the crow who was out late.

" Master at home? "

Guster is minding the shop, for the 'prentices take tea in the kitchen, with Mr. and Mrs. Snagsby; consequently, the robe-maker's two daughters, combing their curls at the two glasses in the two second-floor windows of the opposite house, are not driving the two 'prentices to distraction, as they fondly suppose, but are merely awakening the unprofitable admiration of Guster, whose hair won't grow, and never would, and, it is confidently thought, never will.

"Master at home?" says Mr. Tulkinghorn.

Master is at home, and Guster will fetch him. Guster disappears, glad to get out of the shop, which she regards with mingled dread and veneration as a store-house of awful implements of the great torture of the law: a place not to be entered after the gas is turned off.

Mr. Snagsby appears: greasy, warm, herbaceous, and chewing. Bolts a bit of bread and butter. Says, "Bless my soul, sir! Mr. Tulkinghorn!"

"I want half a word with you, Snagsby."

"Certainly, sir! Dear me, sir, why didn't you send your young man round for me? Pray walk into the back shop, sir." Snagsby has brightened in a moment.

The confined room, strong of parchment-grease, is warehouse, counting-house, and copying-office. Mr. Tulkinghorn sits, facing round, on a stool at the desk.

"Jarndyce and Jarndyce, Snagsby."

"Yes, sir." Mr. Snagsby turns up the gas, and coughs behind his hand, modestly anticipating profit. Mr. Snagsby, as a timid man, is accustomed to cough with a variety of expression, and so to save words.

"You copied some affidavits in that cause for me lately."

"Yes, sir, we did."

"There was one of them," said Mr. Tulkinghorn, carelessly feeling—tight, unopenable Oyster of the old school!—in the wrong coat-pocket, "the hand-writing of which is peculiar, and I rather like it. As I happened to be passing, and thought I had it about me, I looked in to ask you—but I haven't got it. No matter, any other time will do—Ah! here it is!—I looked in to ask you who copied this?"

"Who copied this, sir?" says Mr. Snagsby, taking it, laying it flat on the desk, and separating all the sheets

23

at once with a twirl and a twist of the left hand peculiar to law-stationers. "We gave this out, sir. We were giving out rather a large quantity of work just at that time. I can tell you in a moment who copied it, sir, by referring to my book."

Mr. Snagsby takes his book down from the safe, makes another bolt of the bit of bread and butter which seemed to have stopped short, eyes the affidavit aside, and brings his right forefinger traveling down a page of the book. "Jewby—Packer—Jarndyce."

"Jarndyce! Here we are, sir," says Mr. Snagsby. "To be sure! I might have remembered it. This was given out, sir, to a writer who lodges just over on the opposite side of the lane."

Mr. Tulkinghorn has seen the entry, found it before the law-stationer, read it while the forefinger was coming down the hill.

"*What* do you call him? Nemo?" says Mr. Tulkinghorn.

"Nemo, sir. Here it is. Forty-two folio. Given out on the Wednesday night, at eight o'clock; brought in on the Thursday morning, at half after nine."

"Nemo!" repeats Mr. Tulkinghorn. "Nemo is Latin for no one."

"It must be English for some one, sir, I think," Mr. Snagsby submits, with his deferential cough. "It is a person's name. Here it is, you see, sir! Forty-two folio. Given out Wednesday night, eight o'clock; brought in Thursday morning, half after nine."

The tail of Mr. Snagsby's eye becomes conscious of the head of Mrs. Snagsby looking in at the shop-door to know what he means by deserting his tea. Mr. Snagsby addresses an explanatory cough to Mrs. Snagsby, as who should say, "My dear, a customer!"

"Half after nine, sir," repeats Mr. Snagsby. "Our law-writers, who live by job-work, are a queer lot; and this may not be his name, but it's the name he goes by. I remember now, sir, that he gives it in a written advertisement he sticks up down at the Rule Office, and the King's Bench Office, and the Judges' Chambers, and so forth. You know the kind of document, sir—wanting employ?"

Mr. Tulkinghorn glances through the little window at the back of Coavinses', the sheriff's officer's, where lights shine in Coavinses' windows. Coavinses' coffee-room is at the back, and the shadows of several gentlemen under a cloud loom cloudily upon the blinds. Mr. Snagsby takes the opportunity of slightly turning his head, to glance over his shoulder at his little woman, and to make apologetic motions with his mouth to this effect: " Tul-king-horn—rich —in-flu-en-tial!"

" Have you given this man work before?" asks Mr. Tulkinghorn.

" O dear, yes, sir! Work of yours."

" Thinking of more important matters, I forget where you said he lived?"

" Across the lane, sir. In fact, he lodges at a—" Mr. Snagsby makes another bolt, as if the bit of bread-and-butter were insurmountable—" at a rag and bottle shop."

" Can you show me the place as I go back?"

" With the greatest pleasure, sir!"

Mr. Snagsby pulls off his sleeves and his gray coat, pulls on his black coat, takes his hat from its peg. " Oh! here is my little woman!" he says aloud. " My dear, will you be so kind as to tell one of the lads to look after the shop, while I step across the lane with Mr. Tulkinghorn? Mrs. Snagsby, sir—I shan't be two minutes, my love!"

Mrs. Snagsby bends to the lawyer, retires behind the counter, peeps at them through the window-blind, goes softly into the back office, refers to the entries in the book still lying open. Is evidently curious.

" You will find that the place is rough, sir," says Mr. Snagsby, walking deferentially in the road, and leaving the narrow pavement to the lawyer; " and the party is very rough. But they're a wild lot in general, sir. The advantage of this particular man is, that he never wants sleep. He'll go at it right on end, if you want him to, as long as ever you like."

Inspector Bucket's Job

It is quite dark, now, and the gas-lamps have acquired their full effect. Jostling against clerks going to post the day's letters, and against counsel and attorneys going home to dinner, and against plaintiffs and defendants, and suitors of all sorts, and against the general crowd, in whose way the forensic wisdom of ages has interposed a million of obstacles to the transaction of the commonest business of life—diving through law and equity, and through that kindred mystery, the street mud, which is made of nobody knows what, and collects about us nobody knows whence or how; we only knowing in general that when there is too much of it, we find it necessary to shovel it away—the lawyer and the law-stationer come to a rag and bottle shop, and general emporium of much disregarded merchandise, lying and being in the shadow of the wall of Lincoln's Inn, and kept, as is announced in paint, to all whom it may concern, by one Krook.

"This is where he lives, sir," says the law-stationer.

"This is where he lives, is it?" says the lawyer unconcernedly. "Thank you."

"Are you not going in, sir?"

"No, thank you, no; I am going on to the Fields at present. Good-evening. Thank you!" Mr. Snagsby lifts his hat, and returns to his little woman and his tea.

But Mr. Tulkinghorn does not go on to the Fields at present. He goes a short way, turns back, comes again to the shop of Mr. Krook, and enters it straight. It is dim enough, with a blot-headed candle or so in the windows, and an old man and a cat sitting in the back part by a fire. The old man rises and comes forward, with another blot-headed candle in his hand.

"Pray is your lodger within?"

"Male or female, sir?" says Mr. Krook.

"Male. The person who does copying."

Mr. Krook has eyed his man narrowly. Knows him by sight. Has an indistinct impression of his aristocratic repute.

"Did you wish to see him, sir?"

26

" Yes."

" It's what I seldom do myself," says Mr. Krook with a grin. " Shall I call him down? But it's a weak chance if he'd come, sir!"

" I'll go up to him, then," says Mr. Tulkinghorn.

" Second floor, sir. Take the candle. Up there!" Mr. Krook, with his cat beside him, stands at the bottom of the staircase, looking after Mr. Tulkinghorn. " Hi—hi!" he says, when Mr. Tulkinghorn has nearly disappeared. The lawyer looks down over the hand-rail. The cat expands her wicked mouth, and snarls at him.

" Order, Lady Jane! Behave yourself to visitors, my lady! You know what they say of my lodger?" whispers Krook, going up a step or two.

" What do they say of him?"

" They say he has sold himself to the Enemy; but you and I know better—he don't buy. I'll tell you what, though; my lodger is so black-humored and gloomy, that I believe he'd as soon make that bargain as any other. Don't put him out, sir. That's my advice!"

Mr. Tulkinghorn with a nod goes on his way. He comes to the dark door on the second floor. He knocks, receives no answer, opens it, and accidentally extinguishes his candle in doing so.

The air of the room is almost bad enough to have extinguished it, if he had not. It is a small room, nearly black with soot, and grease, and dirt. In the rusty skeleton of a grate, pinched at the middle as if poverty had gripped it, a red coke fire burns low. In the corner by the chimnew, stand a deal table and a broken desk; a wilderness marked with a rain of ink. In another corner, a ragged old portmanteau on one of the two chairs, serves for cabinet or wardrobe; no larger one is needed, for it collapses like the cheeks of a starved man. The floor is bare; except that one old mat, trodden to shreds of rope-yarn, lies perishing upon the hearth. No curtain veils the darkness of the night, but the discolored shutters are drawn together; and through the two gaunt holes pierced in them, famine might be staring in—the Banshee of the man upon the bed.

For, on a low bed opposite the fire, a confusion of dirty patchwork, lean-ribbed ticking, and coarse sacking, the lawyer, hesitating just within the doorway, sees a man. He lies there, dressed in shirt and trousers, with bare feet. He has a yellow look in the spectral darkness of a candle that has guttered down, until the whole length of its wick (still burning) has doubled over, and left a tower of winding-sheet above it. His hair is ragged, mingling with his whiskers and his beard—the latter, ragged too, and grown, like the scum and mist around him, in neglect. Foul and filthy as the room is, foul and filthy as the air is, it is not easy to perceive what fumes those are which most oppress the senses in it; but through the general sickliness and faintness, and the odor of stale tobacco, there comes into the lawyer's mouth the bitter, vapid taste of opium.

"Hallo, my friend!" he cries, and strikes his iron candle-stick against the door.

He thinks he has awakened his friend. He lies a little turned away, but his eyes are surely open.

"Hallo, my friend!" he cries again. "Hallo! Hallo!"

As he rattles on the door, the candle, which has drooped so long, goes out, and leaves him in the dark; with the gaunt eyes in the shutters staring down upon the bed.

III

OUR DEAR BROTHER

A TOUCH on the lawyer's wrinkled hand, as he stands in the dark room, irresolute, makes him start and say, "What's that?"

"It's me," returns the old man of the house, whose breath is in his ear. "Can't you wake him?"

"No."

"What have you done with your candle?"

"It's gone out. Here it is."

Krook takes it, goes to the fire, stoops over the red embers, and tries to get a light. The dying ashes have no light to spare, and his endeavors are vain. Muttering, after an ineffectual call to his lodger, that he will go downstairs and bring a lighted candle from the shop, the old man departs. Mr. Tulkinghorn, for some new reason that he has, does not await his return in the room, but on the stairs outside.

The welcome light soon shines upon the wall, as Krook comes slowly up, with his green-eyed cat following at his heels. " Does the man generally sleep like this? " inquires the lawyer, in a low voice. " Hi! I don't know," says Krook, shaking his head and lifting his eyebrows. " I know next to nothing of his habits, except that he keeps himself very close."

Thus whispering, they both go in together. As the light goes in, the great eyes in the shutters, darkening, seem to close. Not so the eyes upon the bed.

"God save us!" exclaimed Mr. Tulkinghorn. "He is dead!"

Krook drops the heavy hand he has taken up, so suddenly that the arm swings over the bedside.

They look at one another for a moment.

"Send for some doctor! Call for Miss Flite up the stairs, sir. Here's poison by the bed! Call out for Flite, will you?" says Krook, with his lean hands spread out above the body like a vampire's wings.

Mr. Tulkinghorn hurries to the landing, and calls " Miss Flite! Flite! Make haste, here, whoever you are! Flite!" Krook follows him with his eyes, and, while he is calling, finds opportunity to steal to the old portmanteau, and steal back again.

"Run, Flite, run! The nearest doctor! Run!" So Mr. Krook addresses a crazy little woman, who is his female lodger: who appears and vanishes in a breath: who soon returns, accompanied by a testy medical man, brought from his dinner—with a broad snuffy lip, and a broad Scotch tongue.

"Ey! Bless the hearts o' ye," says the medical man, looking up at them after a moment's examination. "He's just as dead as Phairy!"

Mr. Tulkinghorn (standing by the old portmanteau) inquires if he has been dead any time?

"Any time, sir?" says the medical gentleman. "It's probable he wull have been dead aboot three hours."

"About that time, I should say," observes a dark young man, on the other side of the bed.

"Air you in the maydickle prayfession yourself, sir?" inquires the first.

The dark young man says yes.

"Then I'll just tak' my depairture," replies the other; "for I'm nae gude here!" With which remark, he finishes his brief attendance, and returns to finish his dinner.

The dark young surgeon passes the candle across and across the face, and carefully examines the law-writer, who has established his pretentions to his name by becoming indeed No one.

"I knew this person by sight, very well," says he. "He has purchased opium of me, for the last year and a half. Was anybody present related to him?" glancing round upon the three bystanders.

"I was his landlord," grimly answers Krook, taking the candle from the surgeon's outstretched hand. "He told me once, I was the nearest relation he had."

"He has died," says the surgeon, "of an over-dose of opium, there is no doubt. The room is strongly flavored with it. There is enough here now," taking an old tea-pot from Mr. Krook, "to kill a dozen people."

"Do you think he did it on purpose?" asks Krook.

"Took the over-dose?"

"Yes!" Krook almost smacks his lips with the unction of a horrible interest.

"I can't say. I should think it unlikely, as he has been in the habit of taking so much. But nobody can tell. He was very poor, I suppose?"

"I suppose he was. His room—don't look rich," says

Krook, who might have changed eyes with his cat, as he casts his sharp glance around. " But I have never been in it since he had it, and he was too close to name his circumstances to me."

" Did he owe you any rent? "

" Six weeks."

" He will never pay it! " says the young man, resuming his examination. " It is beyond a doubt that he is indeed as dead as Pharaoh; and to judge from his appearance and condition, I should think it a happy release. Yet he must have been a good figure when a youth, and I dare say, good-looking." He says this, not unfeelingly, while sitting on the bedstead's edge, with his face towards that other face, and his hand upon the region of the heart. " I recollect once thinking there was something in his manner, uncouth as it was, that denoted a fall in life. Was that so? " he continues, looking round.

Krook replies, " You might as well ask me to describe the ladies whose heads of hair I have got in sacks downstairs. Than that he was my lodger for a year and a half, and lived—or didn't live—by law-writing, I know no more of him."

During this dialogue, Mr. Tulkinghorn has stood aloof by the old portmanteau, with his hands behind him, equally removed, to all appearance, from all three kinds of interest exhibited near the bed—from the young surgeon's professional interest in death, noticeable as being quite apart from his remarks on the deceased as an individual; from the old man's unction; and the little crazy woman's awe. His imperturbable face has been as inexpressive as his rusty clothes. One could not even say he has been thinking all this while. He has shown neither patience nor impatience, nor attention nor abstraction. He has shown nothing but his shell. As easily might the tone of a delicate musical instrument be inferred from its case, as the tone of Mr. Tulkinghorn from *his* case.

He now interposes; addressing the young surgeon, in his unmoved, professional way.

"I looked in here," he observes, "just before you, with the intention of giving this deceased man, whom I never saw alive, some employment at his trade of copying. I had heard of him from my stationer—Snagsby of Cook's Court. Since no one here knows anything about him, it might be as well to send for Snagsby. Ah!" to the little crazy woman, who has often seen him in court, and whom he has often seen, and who proposes, in frightened dumb-show, to go for the law-stationer. "Suppose you do!"

While she is gone, the surgeon abandons his hopeless investigation, and covers its subject with the patchwork counterpane. Mr. Krook and he interchange a word or two. Mr. Tulkinghorn says nothing; but stands, ever, near the old portmanteau.

Mr. Snagsby arrives hastily, in his gray coat and black sleeves. "Dear me, dear me," he says; "and it has come to this, has it! Bless my soul!"

"Can you give the person of the house any information about this unfortunate creature, Snagsby?" inquires Mr. Tulkinghorn. "He was in arrears with his rent, it seems. And he must be buried, you know."

"Well, sir," says Mr. Snagsby, coughing his apologetic cough behind his hand; "I really don't know what advice you could offer, except sending for the beadle."

"I don't speak of advice," returns Mr. Tulkinghorn. "*I* could advise——"

"No one better, sir, I am sure," says Mr. Snagsby, with his deferential cough.

"I speak of affording some clew to his connections, or to where he came from, or to anything concerning him."

"I assure you, sir," says Mr. Snagsby, after prefacing his reply with his cough of general propitiation, "that I know no more where he came from than I know——"

"Where he has gone to, perhaps," suggests the surgeon, to help him out.

A pause. Mr. Tulkinghorn looking at the law-stationer. Mr. Krook, with his mouth open, looking for somebody to speak next.

"As to his connections, sir," says Mr. Snagsby, "if a person was to say to me, 'Snagsby, here's twenty thousand pound down, ready for you in the Bank of England, if you'll only name one of them,' I couldn't do it, sir! About a year and a half ago—to the best of my belief at the time when he first came to lodge at the present rag and bottle shop——"

"That was the time!" says Krook, with a nod.

"About a year and a half ago," says Mr. Snagsby, strengthened, "he came into our place one morning after breakfast, and, finding my little woman (which I name Mrs. Snagsby when I use that appellation) in our shop, produced a specimen of his handwriting, and gave her to understand that he was in want of copying work to do, and was— not to put too fine a point upon it"—a favorite apology for plain-speaking with Mr. Snagsby, which he always offers with a sort of argumentative frankness, "hard up! My little woman is not in general partial to strangers, particular —not to put too fine a point upon it—when they want anything. But she was rather took by something about his person: whether by his being unshaved, or by his hair being in want of attention, or by what other ladies' reasons, I leave you to judge; and she accepted of the specimen, and likewise of the address. My little woman hasn't a good ear for names," proceeds Mr. Snagsby, after consulting his cough of consideration behind his hand, "and she considered Nemo equally the same as Nimrod. In consequence of which, she got into a habit of saying to me at meals, 'Mr. Snagsby, you haven't found Nimrod any work yet?' or 'Mr. Snagsby, why didn't you give that eight-and-thirty Chancery folio in Jarndyce, to Nimrod? or such like. And that is the way he gradually fell into job-work at our place; and that is the most I know of him, except that he was a quick hand, and a hand not sparing of night work; and that if you gave him out, say five-and-forty folio on the Wednesday night, you would have it brought in on the Thursday morning. All of which "—Mr. Snagsby concludes by politely motioning with his hat towards the bed, as much as to add—" I have no doubt my honorable friend would confirm, if he were in a condition to do it."

" Hadn't you better see," says Mr. Tulkinghorn to Krook, " whether he had any papers that may enlighten you? There will be an inquest, and you will be asked the question. You can read? "

" No I can't," returns the old man, with a sudden grin.

" Snagsby," says Mr. Tulkinghorn, " look over the room for him. He will get into some trouble or difficulty, otherwise. Being here, I'll wait, if you make haste; and then I can testify on his behalf, if it should ever be necessary, that all was fair and right. If you will hold the candle for Mr. Snagsby, my friend, he'll soon see whether there is anything to help you."

" In the first place, here's an old portmanteau, sir," says Snagsby.

Ah, to be sure, so there is! Mr. Tulkinghorn does not appear to have seen it before, though he is standing so close to it, and though there is very little else, Heaven knows.

The marine-store merchant holds the light, and the law stationer conducts the search. The surgeon leans against the corner of the chimney-piece; Miss Flite peeps and trembles just within the door. The apt old scholar of the old school, with his dull black breeches tied with ribbons at the knees, his large black waistcoat, his long-sleeved black coat, and his wisp of limp white neckerchief tied in the bow the Peerage knows so well, stands in exactly the same place and attitude.

There are some worthless articles of clothing in the old portmanteau; there is a bundle of pawnbrokers' duplicates, those turnpike tickets on the road of Poverty; there is a crumpled paper smelling of opium, on which are scrawled rough memoranda—as, took, such a day, so many grains; took, such another day, so many more—begun some time ago, as if with the intention of being regularly continued, but soon left off. There are a few dirty scraps of newspapers, all referrring to Coroners' Inquests; there is nothing else. They search the cupboard, and the drawer of the ink-splashed table. There is not a morsel of an old letter, or of any other writing, in either. The young surgeon examines the dress on the law-writer. A knife and some odd half-pence are all he finds. Mr. Snagsby's suggestion is the practical suggestion after all, and the beadle must be called in.

So the little crazy lodger goes for the beadle, and the rest come out of the room. "Don't leave the cat there!" says the surgeon: "that won't do!" Mr. Krook therefore drives her out before him; and she goes furtively downstairs, winding her little tail, and licking her lips.

"Good-night!" says Mr. Tulkinghorn; and goes home to Allegory and meditation.

IV

THE CORONER'S JURY

MR. TULKINGHORN is received with distinction, and seated near the Coroner; between that high judicial officer, a bagatelle-board, and the coal-box. The inquiry proceeds. The Jury learn how the subject of their inquiry died, and learn no more about him. "A very eminent solicitor is in attendance, gentlemen," says the Coroner, "who, I am informed, was accidentally present, when discovery of the death was made; but he could only repeat the evidence you have already heard from the surgeon, the landlord, the lodger, and the law-stationer; and it is not necessary to trouble him. Is anybody in attendance who knows anything more?"

Mrs. Piper pushed forward by Mrs. Perkins, Mrs. Piper sworn.

Anastasia Piper, gentlemen. Married woman. Now, Mrs. Piper—what have you to say about this?

Why, Mrs. Piper has a good deal to say, chiefly in parenthesis and without punctuation, but not much to tell. Mrs. Piper lives in the court (which her husband is a cabinet-maker), and it has long been well beknown among the neighbors (counting from the day next but one before the half-baptizing of Alexander James Piper aged eighteen months and four days old on accounts of not being expected to live such was the sufferings gentlemen of that child in his gums) as the Plaintive—so Mrs. Piper insists on calling the deceased—was reported to have sold himself. Thinks it was the Plaintive's air in which that report originatinin. See the Plaintive often and considered as his air was feariocious and not to be allowed to go about some children being timid (and if doubted hoping Mrs. Perkins may be brought forard for she is here and will do credit to her husband and herself and family). Has seen the Plaintive wexed and worrited by the children (for children they will ever be and you cannot expect them specially if of playful dispositions to be Methoozellers which you was not yourself). On accounts of this and his dark looks has often dreamed as she see him take a pick-axe from his pocket and split Johnny's head (which the child knows not fear and has repeatually called after him close at his eels). Never however see the Plaintive take a pick-axe or any other wepping far from it. Has seen him hurry away when run and called after as if not partial to children and never see him speak to neither child nor grown person at any time (excepting the boy that sweeps the crossing down the lane over the way round the corner which if he was here would tell you that he has been a-speaking to him frequent).

Says the Coroner, is that boy here? Says the beadle, no, sir, he is not here. Says the Coroner, go and fetch him then. In the absence of the active and intelligent, the Coroner converses with Mr. Tulkinghorn.

O! Here's the boy, gentlemen!

Here he is, very muddy, very hoarse, very ragged. Now, boy!—But stop a minute. Caution. This boy must be put through a few preliminary paces.

Name, Jo. Nothing else that he knows on. Don't know that everybody has two names. Never heerd of such a think. Don't know that Jo is short for a longer name. Thinks it long enough for *him*. *He* don't find no fault with it. Spell it? No. *He* can't spell it. No father, no mother, no friends. Never been to school. What's home? Knows a broom's a broom, and knows it's wicked to tell a lie. Don't recollect who told him about the broom, or about the lie, but knows both. Can't exactly say what'll be done to him arter he's dead if he tells a lie to the gentlemen here, but believes it'll be something wery bad to punish him, and serve him right—and so he'll tell you the truth.

" This won't do, gentlemen! " says the Coroner, with a melancholy shake of the head.

" Don't you think you can receive his evidence, sir? " asks an attentive Juryman.

" Out of the question," says the Coroner. " You have heard the boy. ' Can't exactly say' won't do, you know. We can't take *that,* in a Court of Justice, gentlemen. It's terrible depravity. Put the boy aside."

Boy put aside; to the great edification of the audience;—especially of Little Swills, the Comic Vocalist.

Now. Is there any other witness? No other witness.

Very well, gentlemen! Here's a man unknown, proved to have been in the habit of taking opium in large quantities for a year and a half, found dead of too much opium. If you think you have any evidence to lead you to the conclusion that he committed suicide, you will come to that conclusion. If you think it is a case of accidental death, you will find a Verdict accordingly.

Verdict accordingly. Accidental death. No doubt. Gentlemen, you are discharged. Good afternoon.

While the Coroner buttons his great-coat, Mr. Tulkinghorn and he give private audience to the rejected witness in a corner.

That graceless creature only knows that the dead man (whom he recognized just now by his yellow face and black hair) was sometimes hooted and pursued about the streets. That one cold, winter night, when he, the boy, was shivering in a doorway near his crossing, the man turned to look at him, and came back, and, having questioned him and found that he had not a friend in the world, said, " Neither have

I. Not one!" and gave him the price of a supper and a night's lodging. That the man had often spoken to him since; and asked him whether he slept sound at night, and how he bore cold and hunger, and whether he ever wished to die; and similar strange questions. That when the man had no money, he would say in passing, "I am as poor as you to-day, Jo," but that when he had any, he had always (as the boy most heartily believes) been glad to give him some.

"He wos wery good to me," says the boy, wiping his eyes with his wretched sleeves. "Wen I see him a-layin' so stritched out just now, I wished he could have heerd me tell him so. He wos wery wood to me, he wos!"

As he shuffles downstairs, Mr. Snagsby, lying in wait for him, puts a half-crown in his hand. "If you ever see me coming past your crossing with my little woman—I mean a lady—" says Mr. Snagsby, with his finger on his nose, "don't allude to it!"

It is anything but a night of rest at Mr. Snagsby's, in Cook's Court; where Guster murders sleep, by going, as Mr. Snagsby himself allows—not to put too fine a point upon it—out of one fit into twenty. The occasion of this seizure is, that Guster has a tender heart, and a susceptible something that possibly might have been imagination but for Tooting and her patron saint. Be it what it may, now, it was so direfully impressed at tea-time by Mr. Snagsby's account of the inquiry at which he had assisted, that at supper-time she projected herself into the kitchen, preceded by a flying Dutch-cheese, and well into a fit of unusual duration: which she only came out of to go into another, and another, and so on through a chain of fits, with short intervals between, of which she has pathetically availed herself by consuming them in entreaties to Mrs. Snagsby not to give her warning "when she quite comes to;" and also in appeals to the whole establishment to lay her down on the stones, and go to bed. Hence, Mr. Snagsby, at last hearing the cock at the little dairy in Cursitor Street go into that disinterested ecstasy of his on the subject of daylight, says, drawing a long breath, though the most patient of men, " I thought you was dead, I am sure !"

What question this enthusiastic fowl supposes he settles when he strains himself to such an extent, or why he should thus crow (so men crow on various triumphant public occasions, however) about what cannot be of any moment to him, is his affair. It is enough that daylight comes, morning comes, noon comes.

Then the active and intelligent, who has got into the morning papers as such, comes with his pauper company to Mr. Krook's, and bears off the body of our dear brother here departed, to a hemmed-in churchyard, pestiferous and obscene, whence malignant diseases are communicated to the bodies of our dear brothers and sisters who have not departed; while our dear brothers and sisters who hang about official back-stairs—would to Heaven they *had* departed !—are very complacent and agreeable. Into a beastly scrap of ground which a Turk would reject as a savage abomination, and a Caffre would shudder at, they bring our dear brother here departed, to receive Christian burial.

With houses looking on, on every side, save where a reeking little tunnel of a court gives access to the iron gate—with every villainy of life in action close on death, and every poisonous element of death in action close on life—here, they lower our dear brother down a foot or two: here, sow him in corruption, to be raised in corruption: an avenging ghost at many a sick-bedside; a shameful testimony to future ages, how civilization and barbarism walked this boastful island together.

Come night, come darkness, for you cannot come too soon, or stay too long, by such a place as this ! Come, straggling lights into the windows of the ugly houses; and you who do iniquity therein, do it at least with this dread scene shut out ! Come, flame of gas, burning so sullenly above the iron gate, on which the poisoned air deposits its witch-ointment slimy to the touch ! It is well that you should call to every passer-by, "Look here !"

With the night, comes a slouching figure through the

tunnel-court, to the outside of the iron gate. It holds the gate with its hands, and looks in between the bars; stands looking in, for a little while.

It then, with an old broom it carries, softly sweeps the step, and makes the archway clean. It does so, very busily and trimly; looks in again, a little while; and so departs.

Jo, is it thou? Well, well! Though a rejected witness, who " can't exactly say " what will be done to him in greater hands than men's, thou art not quite in outer darkness. There is something like a distant ray of light in thy muttered reason for this:

" He wos wery good to me, he wos! "

V

ON THE WATCH

It has left off raining down in Lincolnshire, at last, and Chesney Wold has taken heart. Mrs. Rouncewell is full of hospitable cares, for Sir Leicester and my Lady are coming home from Paris. The fashionable intelligence has found it out, and communicates the glad tidings to benighted England. It has also found out, that they will entertain a brilliant and distinguished circle of the *élite* of the *beau monde* (the fashionable intelligence is weak in English, but a giant refreshed in French), at the ancient and hospitable family seat in Lincolnshire.

For the greater honor of the brilliant and distinguished circle, and of Chesney Wold into the bargain, the broken arch of the bridge in the park is mended; and the water, now retired within its proper limits and again spanned gracefully, makes a figure in the prospect from the house. The clear, cold sunshine glances into the brittle woods, and approvingly beholds the sharp wind scattering the leaves and drying the moss. It glides over the park after the moving shadows of the clouds, and chases them, and never catches them, all day. It looks in at the windows, and touches the ancestral portraits with bars and patches of brightness, never contemplated by the painters. Athwart the picture of my Lady, over the great chimney-piece, it throws a broad bend-sinister of light that strikes down crookedly into the hearth, and seems to rend it.

Through the same cold sunshine, and the same sharp wind, my Lady and Sir Leicester, in their traveling chariot (my Lady's woman, and Sir Leicester's man affectionate in the rumble), start for home. With a considerable amount of jingling and whip-cracking, and many plunging demonstrations on the part of two bare-backed horses, and two Centaurs with glazed hats, jack-boots, and flowing manes and tails, they rattle out of the yard of the Hôtel Bristol in the Place Vendôme, and canter between the sun-and-shadow-chequered colonnade of the Rue de Rivoli and the garden of the ill-fated palace of a headless king and queen, off by the Place of Concord, and the Elysian Fields, and the Gate of the Star, out of Paris.

Sooth to say, they cannot go away too fast; for, even here, my Lady Dedlock has been bored to death. Concert, assembly, opera, theatre, drive, nothing is new to my Lady, under the worn-out heavens. Only last Sunday, when poor wretches were gay—within the walls, playing with children among the clipped trees and the statues in the Palace Garden; walking, a score abreast, in the Elysian Fields, made more Elysian by performing dogs and wooden horses; between whiles filtering (a few) through the gloomy Cathedral of our Lady, to say a word or two at the base of a pillar, within flare of a rusty little gridironfull of gusty little tapers—without the walls, encompassing Paris with dancing, love-making, wine-drinking, tobacco-smoking, tomb-visiting, billiard, card and domino playing, quack-doctoring, and much murderous refuse, animate and inanimate, only last Sunday, my Lady, in the desolation of Boredom and the clutch of Giant Despair, almost hated her own maid for being in spirits.

She cannot, therefore, go too fast from Paris. Weariness of soul lies before her, as it lies behind—her Ariel has put a girdle of it round the whole earth, and it cannot be unclasped—but the imperfect remedy is always to fly, from the last place where it has been experienced. Fling Paris back into the distance, then, exchanging it for endless avenues and cross-avenues of wintry trees! And, when next beheld, let it be some leagues away, with the Gate of the Star a white speck glittering in the sun, and the city a mere mound in a plain; two dark square towers rising out of it, and light and shadow descending on it aslant, like the angels in Jacob's dream!

Sir Leicester is generally in a complacent state, and rarely bored. When he has nothing else to do, he can always contemplate his own greatness. It is a considerable advantage to a man to have so inexhaustible a subject. After reading his letters, he leans back in his corner of the carriage, and generally reviews his importance to society.

"You have an unusual amount of correspondence this morning?" says my Lady after a long time. She is fatigued with reading. Has almost read a page in twenty miles.

"Nothing in it, though. Nothing whatever."

"I saw one of Mr. Tulkinghorn's long effusions, I think?"

"You see everything," says Sir Leicester, with admiration.

"Ha!" sighs my Lady, "he is the most tiresome of men!"

"He sends—I really beg your pardon—he sends," says Sir Leicester, selecting the letter and unfolding it, "a message to you. Our stopping to change horses, as I came to his postscript, drove it out of my memory. I beg you'll excuse me. He says——" Sir Leicester is so long in taking out his eye-glass and adjusting it, that my Lady looks a little irritated. "He says, 'In the matter of the right of way——' I beg your pardon, that's not the place. He says—yes! Here I have it! He says, 'I beg my respectful compliments to my Lady, who, I hope, has benefited by the change. Will you do me the favor to mention (as it may interest her) that I have something to tell her on her return, in reference to the person who copied the affidavit in the

Chancery suit, which so powerfully stimulated her curiosity. I have seen him.' "

My Lady, leaning forward, looks out of her window.

" That's the message," observes Sir Leicester.

" I should like to walk a little," says my Lady, still looking out of the window.

" Walk ? " repeats Sir Leicester, in a tone of surprise.

" I should like to walk a little," says my Lady, with unmistakable distinctness. " Please to stop the carriage."

The carriage is stopped, the affectionate man alights from the rumble, opens the door, and lets down the steps, obedient to an impatient motion of my Lady's hand. My Lady alights so quickly, and walks away so quickly, that Sir Leicester, for all his scrupulous politeness, is unable to assist her, and is left behind. A space of a minute or two has elapsed before he comes up with her. She smiles, looks very handsome, takes his arm, lounges with him for a quarter of a mile, is very much bored, and resumes her seat in the carriage.

The rattle and clatter continue through the greater part of three days, with more or less of bell-jingling and whipcracking, and more or less plunging of Centaurs and barebacked horses. Their courtly politeness to each other, at the Hotels where they tarry, is the theme of general admiration. Though my Lord *is* a little aged for my Lady, says Madame, the hostess of the Golden Ape, and though he might be her amiable father, one can see at a glance that they love each other. One observes my Lord with his white hair, standing, hat in hand, to help my Lady, to and from the carriage. One observes my Lady, how recognizant of my Lord's politeness, with an inclination of her gracious head and the concession of her so genteel fingers! It is ravishing!

The sea has no appreciation of great men, but knocks them about like the small fry. It is habitually hard upon Sir Leicester, whose countenance it greenly mottles in the manner of sage-cheese, and in whose aristocratic system it effects a dismal revolution. It is the Radical of Nature to him. Nevertheless, his dignity gets over it, after stopping to refit; and he goes on with my Lady for Chesney Wold, lying only one night in London on the way to Lincolnshire.

Through the same cold sunlight—colder as the day declines,—and through the same sharp wind—sharper as the separate shadows of bare trees gloom together in the woods, and as the Ghost's Walk, touched at the western corner by a pile of fire in the sky, resigns itself to coming night,—they drive into the park. The Rooks, swinging in their lofty houses in the elm-tree avenue, seem to discuss the question of the occupancy of the carriage as it passes underneath; some agreeing that Sir Leicester and my Lady are come down; some arguing with malcontents who won't admit it; now, all consenting to consider the question disposed of; now, all breaking out in violent debate, incited by one obstinate and drowsy bird, who will persist in putting in a last contradictory croak. Leaving them to swing and caw, the traveling chariot rolls on to the house; where fires gleam warmly through some of the windows, though not through so many as to give an inhabited expression to the darkening mass in front. But the brilliant and distinguished circle will soon do that.

Mrs. Rouncewell is in attendance, and receives Sir Leicester's customary shake of the hand with a profound courtesy.

"How do you do, Mrs. Rouncewell? I am glad to see you."

"I hope I have the honor of welcoming you in good health, Sir Leicester?"

"In excellent health, Mrs. Rouncewell."

"My Lady is looking charmingly well," says Mrs. Rouncewell, with another courtesy.

My Lady signifies, without profuse expenditure of words, that she is as wearily well as she can hope to be.

My Lady's maid is a Frenchwoman of two-and-thirty, from somewhere in the southern country about Avignon and Marseilles—a large-eyed brown woman with black hair; who would be handsome, but for a certain feline

44

mouth, and general uncomfortable tightness of the face, rendering the jaws too eager, and the skull too prominent. There is something indefinably keen and wan about her anatomy; and she has a watchful way of looking out of the corners of her eyes without turning her head, which could be pleasantly dispensed with—especially when she is in an ill-humor and near knives. Through all the good taste of her dress and little adornments, these objections so express themselves, that she seems to go about like a very neat She-Wolf imperfectly tamed. Besides being accomplished in all the knowledge appertaining to her post, she is almost an Englishwoman in her acquaintance with the language—consequently, she is in no want of words to shower upon Rosa for having attracted my Lady's attention; and she pours them out with such grim ridicule as she sits at dinner, that her companion, the affectionate man, is rather relieved when she arrives at the spoon stage of that performance.

Ha, ha, ha! She, Hortense, been in my Lady's service since five years, and always kept at the distance, and this doll, this puppet, caressed—absolutely caressed—by my Lady on the moment of her arrival at the house! Ha, ha, ha! "And do you know how pretty you are, child?"—"No, my Lady."—You are right there! "And how old are you, child! And take care they do not spoil you by flattery, child!" O how droll! It is the *best* thing altogether.

In short, it is such an admirable thing, that Mademoiselle Hortense can't forget it; but at meals for days afterwards, even among her countrywomen and others attached in like capacity to the troop of visitors, relapses into silent enjoyment of the joke—an enjoyment expressed, in her own convivial manner, by an additional tightness of face, thin elongation of compressed lips, and sidewise look: which intense appreciation of humor is frequently reflected in my Lady's mirrors, when my Lady is not among them.

All the mirrors in the house are brought into action now: many of them after a long blank. They reflect handsome faces, simpering faces, youthful faces, faces of three-score-

and-ten that will not submit to be old: the entire collection of faces that have come to pass a January week or two at Chesney Wold, and which the fashionable intelligence, a mighty hunter before the Lord, hunts with a keen scent, from their breaking cover at the Court of St. James's to their being run down to Death. The place in Lincolnshire is all alive. By day, guns and voices are heard ringing in the woods, horsemen and carriages enliven the park roads, servants and hangers-on pervade the Village and the Dedlock Arms. Seen by night, from distant openings in the trees, the row of windows in the long drawing-room, where my Lady's picture hangs over the great chimney-piece, is like a row of jewels set in a black frame. On Sunday, the chill little church is almost warmed by so much gallant company, and the general flavor of the Dedlock dust is quenched in delicate perfumes.

The brilliant and distinguished circle comprehends within it no contracted amount of education, sense, courage, honor, beauty, and virtue. Yet there is something a little wrong about it, in despite of its immense advantages. What can it be?

Dandyism? There is no King George the Fourth now (more's the pity!) to set the dandy fashion; there are no clear-starched jack-towel neckcloths, no short-waisted coats, no false calves, no stays. There are no caricatures, now, of effeminate exquisites so arrayed, swooning in operaboxes with excess of delight, and being revived by other dainty creatures, poking long-necked scent bottles at their noses. There is no beau whom it takes four men at once to shake into his buckskins, or who goes to see all the executions, or who is troubled with the self-approach of having once consumed a pea. But is there Dandyism in the brilliant and distinguished circle notwithstanding, Dandyism of a more mischievous sort, that has got below the surface and is doing less harmless things than jack-toweling itself and stopping its own digestion, to which no rational person need particularly object?

Why, yes. It cannot be disguised. There *are*, at Ches-

ney Wold this January week, some ladies and gentlemen
of the newest fashion, who have set up a dandyism—in
religion, for instance. Who, in mere lackadaisical want of
an emotion, have agreed upon a little dandy talk about
the vulgar wanting faith in things in general; meaning, in
the things that have been tried and found wanting, as
though a low fellow should unaccountably lose faith in a
bad shilling, after finding it out! Who would make the
vulgar very picturesque and faithful, by putting back the
hands upon the clock of time, and canceling a few hundred years of history.

There are also ladies and gentlemen of another fashion,
not so new, but very elegant, who have agreed to put a
smooth glaze on the world, and to keep down all its
realities. For whom everything must be languid and
pretty. Who have found out the perpetual stoppage. Who
are to rejoice at nothing, and be sorry for nothing. Who
are not to be disturbed by ideas. On whom even the fine
arts, attending in powder and walking backward like the
Lord Chamberlain, must array themselves in the milliners
and tailors' patterns of past generations, and be particularl,
careful not to be in earnest or to receive any impress from
the moving age.

Then there is my Lord Boodle, of considerable reputation with his party, who has known what office is, and who
tells Sir Leicester Dedlock with much gravity, after dinner,
that he really does not see to what the present age is tend-
ing. A debate is not what a debate used to be; the House
is not what the House used to be; even a Cabinet is not
what it formerly was. He perceives with astonishment,
that supposing the present government be overthrown, the
limited choice of the Crown, in the formation of a new
ministry, would lie between Lord Coodle and Sir Thomas
Doodle—supposing it to be impossible for the Duke of
Foodle to act with Goodle, which may be assumed to be
the case in consequence of the breach arising out of that
affair with Hoodle. Then, giving the Home Department
and the leadership of the House of Commons to Joodle,

the Exchequer to Koodle, the Colonies to Loodle, and the Foreign Office to Moodle, what are you to do with Noodle? You can't offer him the Presidency of the Council; that is reserved for Poodle. You can't put him in the Woods and Forests; that is hardly good enough for Quoodle. What follows? That the country is shipwrecked, lost, and gone to pieces (as is made manifest to the patriotism of Sir Leicester Dedlock), because you can't provide for Noodle!

On the other hand, the Right Honorable William Buffy, M.P., contends across the table with someone else, that the shipwreck of the country—about which there is no doubt; it is only the manner of it that is in question—is attributable to Cuffy. If you had done with Cuffy what you ought to have done when he first came into Parliament, and had prevented him from going over to Duffy, you would have got him into alliance with Fuffy, you would have had with you the weight attaching as a smart debater to Guffy, you would have brought to bear upon the elections the wealth of Huffy, you would have got in for three counties Juffy, Kuffy, and Luffy, and you would have strengthened your administration by the official knowledge and the business habits of Muffy. All this, instead of being as you now are, dependent on the mere caprice of Puffy!

As to this point, and as to some minor topics, there are differences of opinion; but it is perfectly clear to the brilliant and distinguished circle, all round, that nobody is in question but Boodle and his retinue, and Buffy and *his* retinue. These are the great actors for whom the stage is reserved. A people there are, no doubt—a certain large number of supernumeraries, who are to be occasionally addressed, and relied upon for shouts and choruses, as on the theatrical stage; but Boodle and Buffy, their followers and families, their heirs, executors, administrators, and assigns, are the born first-actors, managers, and leaders, and no others can appear upon the scene for ever and ever.

In this, too, there is perhaps more dandyism at Chesney Wold than the brilliant and distinguished circle will find good for itself in the long run. For it is, even with the

stillest and politest circles, as with the circle the necro-
mancer draws around him—very strange appearances may
be seen in active motion outside. With this difference:
that, being realities and not phantoms, there is the greater
danger of their breaking in.

Chesney Wold is quite full, anyhow; so full, that a burning sense of injury arises in the breasts of ill-lodged ladies'-
maids, and is not to be extinguished. Only one room is
empty. It is a turret chamber of the third order of merit,
plainly, but comfortably furnished, and having an old-
fashioned business air. It is Mr. Tulkinghorn's room, and
is never bestowed on anybody else, for he may come at
any time. He is not come yet. It is his quiet habit to
walk across the park from the village in fine weather; to
drop into this room, as if he had never been out of it since
he was last seen there; to request a servant to inform Sir
Leicester that he is arrived, in case he should be wanted;
and to appear ten minutes before dinner, in the shadow
of the library-door. He sleeps in his turret, with a complaining flag-staff over his head; and has some leads outside, on which, any fine morning when he is down here,
his black figure may be seen walking before breakfast like
a larger species of rook.

Every day before dinner, my Lady looks for him in the
dusk of the library, but he is not there. Every day at
dinner, my Lady glances down the table for the vacant
place, that would be waiting to receive him if he had just
arrived; but there is no vacant place. Every night, my
Lady casually asks her maid:

" Is Mr. Tulkinghorn come? "

Every night the answer is, " No, my Lady, not yet."

One night, while having her hair undressed, my Lady
loses herself in deep thought after this reply, until she sees
her own brooding face, in the opposite glass, and a pair
of black eyes curiously observing her.

" Be so good as to attend," says my Lady then, addressing the reflection of Hortense, " to your business. You
can contemplate your beauty at another time."

49

"Pardon! It was your Ladyship's beauty."

"That," says my Lady, "you needn't contemplate at all."

At length, one afternoon a little before sunset, when the bright groups of figures, which have for the last hour or two enlivened the Ghost's Walk, are all dispersed, and only Sir Leicester and my Lady remain upon the terrace, Mr. Tulkinghorn appears. He comes towards them at his usual methodical pace, which is never quickened, never slackened. He wears his usual expressionless mask—if it be a mask—and carries family secrets in every limb of his body, and every crease of his dress. Whether his whole soul is devoted to the great, or whether he yields them nothing beyond the services he sells, is his personal secret. He keeps it, as he keeps the secrets of his clients; he is his own client in that matter, and will never betray himself.

"How do you do, Mr. Tulkinghorn?" says Sir Leicester, giving him his hand.

Mr. Tulkinghorn is quite well. Sir Leicester is quite well. My Lady is quite well. All highly satisfactory. The lawyer, with his hands behind him, walks, at Sir Leicester's side, along the terrace. My Lady walks upon the other side.

"We expected you before," says Sir Leicester. A gracious observation. As much as to say, "Mr. Tulkinghorn, we remember your existence when you are not here to remind us of it by your presence. We bestow a fragment of our minds upon you, sir, you see!"

Mr. Tulkinghorn, comprehending it, inclines his head, and says he is much obliged.

"I should have come down sooner," he explains, "but that I have been much engaged with those matters in the several suits between yourself and Boythorn."

"A man of a very ill-regulated mind," observes Sir Leicester, with severity. "An extremely dangerous person in any community. A man of a very low character of mind."

"He is obstinate," says Mr. Tulkinghorn.

"It is natural to such a man to be so," says Sir Leicester, looking most profoundly obstinate himself. "I am not at all surprised to hear it."

"The only question is," pursues the lawyer, "whether you will give up anything."

"No, sir," replies Sir Leicester. "Nothing. *I* give up?"

"I don't mean anything of importance. That, of course, I know you would not abandon. I mean any minor point."

"Mr. Tulkinghorn," returns Sir Leicester, "there can be no minor point between myself and Mr. Boythorn. If I go farther, and observe that I cannot readily conceive how *any* right of mine can be a minor point, I speak not so much in reference to myself as an individual, as in reference to the family position I have it in charge to maintain."

Mr. Tulkinghorn inclines his head again. "I have now my instructions," he says. "Mr. Boythorn will give us a good deal of trouble——"

"It is the character of such a mind, Mr. Tulkinghorn," Sir Leicester interrupts him, "*to* give trouble. An exceedingly ill-conditioned, leveling person. A person who, fifty years ago, would probably have been tried at the Old Bailey for some demagogue proceeding, and severely punished—if not," adds Sir Leicester, after a moment's pause, "if not hanged, drawn, and quartered."

Sir Leicester appears to discharge his stately breast of a burden, in passing this capital sentence; as if it were the next satisfactory thing to have the sentence executed.

"But night is coming on," says he, "and my Lady will take cold. My dear, let us go in."

As they turn towards the hall-door, Lady Dedlock addresses Mr. Tulkinghorn for the first time.

"You sent me a message respecting the person whose writing I happened to inquire about. It was like you to remember the circumstance; I had quite forgotten it. Your message reminded me of it again. I can't imagine what association I had with a hand like that; but I surely had some."

"You had some?" Mr. Tulkinghorn repeats.

"O yes!" returns my Lady carelessly. "I think I

must have had some. And did you really take the trouble to find out the writer of that actual thing—what is it!—affidavit?"

"Yes."

"How very odd!"

They pass into a somber breakfast-room on the ground floor, lighted in the day by two deep windows. It is now twilight. The fire glows brightly on the paneled wall, and palely on the window-glass, where, through the cold reflection of the blaze, the colder landscape shudders in the wind, and a gray mist creeps along: the only traveler besides the waste of clouds.

My Lady lounges in a great chair in the chimney-corner, and Sir Leicester takes another great chair opposite. The lawyer stands before the fire, with his hand at arm's length, shading his face. He looks across his arm at my Lady.

"Yes," he says, "I inquired about the man, and found him. And, what is very strange, I found him——"

"Not to be any out-of-the-way person, I am afraid!" Lady Dedlock anticipates.

"I found him dead."

"O dear me!" remonstrated Sir Leicester. Not so much shocked by the fact, as by the fact of the fact being mentioned.

"I was directed to his lodging—a miserable, poverty-stricken place—and I found him dead."

"You will excuse me, Mr. Tulkinghorn," observes Sir Leicester. "I think the less said——"

"Pray, Sir Leicester, let me hear the story out" (it is my Lady speaking). "It is quite a story for twilight. How very shocking! Dead?"

Mr. Tulkinghorn re-asserts it by another inclination of his head. "Whether by his own hand——"

"Upon my honor!" cries Sir Leicester. "Really!"

"Do let me hear the story!" says my Lady.

"Whatever you desire, my dear. But, I must say——"

"No, you mustn't say! Go on, Mr. Tulkinghorn."

Sir Leicester's gallantry concedes the point; though he still feels that to bring this sort of squalor among the upper classes is really—really——

"I was about to say," resumes the lawyer, with undisturbed calmness, "that whether he had died by his own hand or not, it was beyond my power to tell you. I should amend that phrase, however, by saying that he had unquestionably died of his own act, though whether by his own deliberate intention, or by mischance, can never certainly be known. The coroner's jury found that he took the poison accidentally."

"And what kind of man," my Lady asks, "was this deplorable creature?"

"Very difficult to say," returns the lawyer, shaking his head. "He had lived so wretchedly, and was so neglected, with his gypsy color, and his wild black hair and beard, that I should have considered him the commonest of the common. The surgeon had a notion that he had once been something better, both in appearance and condition."

"What did they call the wretched being?"

"They called him what he had called himself, but no one knew his name."

"Not even anyone who had attended on him?"

"No one had attended on him. He was found dead. In fact, I found him."

"Without any clew to anything more?"

"Without any; there was," says the lawyer meditatively, "an old portmanteau; but—No, there were no papers."

During the utterance of every word of this short dialogue, Lady Dedlock and Mr. Tulkinghorn, without any other alteration in their customary deportment, have looked very steadily at one another—as was natural, perhaps, in the discussion of so unusual a subject. Sir Leicester has looked at the fire, with the general expression of the Dedlock on the staircase. The story being told, he renews his stately protest, saying, that as it is quite clear that no association in my Lady's mind can possibly be traceable to this poor wretch (unless he was a begging letter writer);

he trusts to hear no more about a subject so far removed from my Lady's station.

"Certainly, a collection of horrors," says my Lady, gathering up her mantles and furs; "but they interest one for the moment! Have the kindness, Mr. Tulkinghorn, to open the door for me."

Mr. Tulkinghorn does so with deference, and holds it open while she passes out. She passes close to him, with her usual fatigued manner, and insolent grace. They meet again at dinner—again, next day—again for many days in succession. Lady Dedlock is always the same exhausted deity, surrounded by worshipers, and terribly liable to be bored to death, even while presiding at her own shrine. Mr. Tulkinghorn is always the same speechless repository of noble confidences: so oddly out of place, and yet so perfectly at home. They appear to take as little note of one another, as any two people, inclosed within the same walls, could. But, whether each evermore watches and suspects the other, evermore mistrustful of some great reservation; whether each is evermore prepared at all points for the other, and never to be taken unawares; what each would give to know how much the other knows—all this is hidden, for the time, in their own hearts.

VI

TOM-ALL-ALONE'S

My Lady Dedlock is restless, very restless. The astonished fashionable intelligence hardly knows where to have her. To-day, she is at Chesney Wold; yesterday she was at her house in town; to-morrow, she may be abroad, for anything the fashionable intelligence can with confidence predict. Even Sir Leicester's gallantry has some trouble to keep pace with her. It would have more, but that his other faithful ally, for better and for worse—the gout—darts into the old oak bed-chamber at Chesney Wold, and grips him by both legs.

54

Sir Leicester receives the gout as a troublesome demon, but still a demon of the patrician order. All the Dedlocks, in the direct male line, through a course of time during and beyond which the memory of man goeth not to the contrary, have had the gout. It can be proved, sir. Other men's fathers may have died of the rheumatism, or may have taken base contagion from the tainted blood of the sick vulgar, but the Dedlock family have communicated something exclusive, even to the leveling process of dying, by dying of their own family gout. It has come down, through the illustrious line, like the plate, or the pictures, or the place in Lincolnshire. It is among their dignities. Sir Leicester is, perhaps, not wholly without an impression, though he has never resolved it into words, that the angel of death in the discharge of his necessary duties may observe to the shades of the aristocracy, " My lords and gentlemen, I have the honor to present to you another Dedlock certified to have arrived per the family gout."

Hence, Sir Leicester yields up his family legs to the family disorder, as if he held his name and fortune on that feudal tenure. He feels, that for a Dedlock to be laid upon his back and spasmodically twitched and stabbed in his extremities is a liberty taken somewhere; but, he thinks, " We have all yielded to this; it belongs to us; it has, for some hundreds of years, been understood that we are not to make the vaults in the park interesting on more ignoble terms; and I submit myself to the compromise."

And a goodly show he makes, lying in a flush of crimson and gold, in the midst of the great drawing-room, before his favorite picture of my Lady, with broad strips of sunlight shining in, down the long perspective, through the long line of windows, and alternating with soft reliefs of shadow. Outside, the stately oaks, rooted for ages in the green ground which has never known ploughshare, but was still a Chase when kings rode to battle with sword and shield, and rode a-hunting with bow and arrow; bear witness to his greatness. Inside, his forefathers, looking on him, from the walls, say, " Each of us was a passing reality here,

55

and left this colored shadow of himself, and melted into remembrance as dreamy as the distant voices of the rooks now lulling you to rest;" and bear their testimony to his greatness, too. And he is very great, this day. And woe to Boythorn, or other daring wight, who shall presumptuously contest an inch with him!

My Lady is at present represented, near Sir Leicester, by her portrait. She has flitted away to town, with no intention of remaining there, and will soon flit hither again, to the confusion of the fashionable intelligence. The house in town is not prepared for her reception. It is muffled and dreary. Only one Mercury in powder, gapes disconsolate at the hall-window; and he mentioned last night to another Mercury of his acquaintance, also accustomed to good society, that if that sort of thing was to last—which it couldn't, for a man of his spirits couldn't bear it, and a man of his figure couldn't be expected to bear it—there would be no resource for him, upon his honor, but to cut his throat!

What connection can there be, between the place in Lincolnshire, the house in town, the Mercury in powder, and the whereabout of Jo the outlaw with the broom, who had that distant ray of light upon him when he swept the churchyard-step? What connection can there have been between many people in the innumerable histories of this world, who, from opposite sides of great gulfs, have, nevertheless, been very curiously brought together!

Jo sweeps his crossing all day long, unconscious of the link, if any link there be. He sums up his mental condition, when asked a question, by replying that he " don't know nothink." He knows that it's hard to keep the mud off the crossing in dirty weather, and harder still to live by doing it. Nobody taught him even that much; he found it out.

Jo lives—that is to say, Jo has not yet died—in a ruinous place, known to the like of him by the name of Tom-all-Alone's. It is a black, dilapidated street, avoided by all decent people; where the crazy houses were seized upon, when their decay was far advanced, by some bold vagrants, who, after establishing their own possession, took to letting them out in lodgings. Now, these tumbling tenements contain, by night, a swarm of misery. As, on the ruined human wretch, vermin parasites appear, so, these ruined shelters have bred a crowd of foul existence that crawls in and out of gaps in walls and boards; and coils itself to sleep, in maggot numbers, where the rain drips in; and comes and goes, fetching and carrying fever, and sowing more evil in its every footprint than Lord Coodle, and Sir Thomas Doodle, and the Duke of Foodle, and all the fine gentlemen in office down to Zoodle, shall set right in five hundred years—though born expressly to do it.

Twice, lately, there has been a crash and a cloud of dust, like the springing of a mine, in Tom-all-Alone's; and, each time, a house has fallen. These accidents have made a paragraph in the newspapers, and have filled a bed or two in the nearest hospital. The gaps remain, and there are not unpopular lodgings among the rubbish. As several more houses are ready to go, the next crash in Tom-all-Alone's may be expected to be a good one.

This desirable property is in Chancery, of course. It would be an insult to the discernment of any man with half an eye, to tell him so. Whether " Tom " is the popular representative of the original plaintiff or defendant in Jarndyce and Jarndyce; or, whether Tom lived here when the suit had laid the street waste, all alone, until other settlers came to join him; or, whether the traditional title is a comprehensive name for a retreat cut off from honest company and put out of the pale of hope; perhaps nobody knows. Certainly, Jo don't know.

" For *I* don't," says Jo, " *I* don't know nothink."

It must be a strange state to be like Jo! To shuffle through the streets, unfamiliar with the shapes, and in utter darkness as to the meaning of those mysterious symbols, so abundant over the shops, and at corners of the streets, and on the doors, and in the windows! To see people read, and to see people write, and to see the postman deliver

letters, and not to have the least idea of all that language—
to be, to every scrap of it, stone blind and dumb! It must
be very puzzling to see the good company going to the
churches on Sundays, with their books in their hands, and
to think (for perhaps Jo *does* think at odd times) what
does it all mean, and if it means anything to anybody, how
comes it that it means nothing to me? To be hustled, and
jostled, and moved on; and really to feel that it would
appear to be perfectly true that I have no business, here
or there, or anywhere; and yet to be perplexed by the consideration that I *am* here somehow, too, and everybody
overlooked me until I became the creature that I am! It
must be a strange state, not merely to be told that I am
scarcely human (as in the case of my offering myself for
a witness), but to feel it of my own knowledge all my life!
To see the horses, dogs, and cattle go by me, and to know
that in ignorance I belong to them, and not the superior
beings in my shape, whose delicacy I offend! Jo's ideas
of a criminal trial, or a judge, or a bishop, or a government, or that inestimable jewel to him (if he only knew it)
the Constitution, should be strange! His whole material,
and immaterial life is wonderfully strange; his death, the
strangest thing of all.

Jo comes out of Tom-all-Alone's, meeting the tardy
morning which is always late in getting down there, and
munches his dirty bit of bread as he comes along. His
way lying through many streets, and the houses not yet
being open, he sits down to breakfast on the doorstep of
the Society for the Propagation of the Gospel in Foreign
Parts, and gives it a brush when he has finished, as an
acknowledgment of the accommodation. He admires the
size of the edifice, and wonders what it's all about. He
has no idea, poor wretch, of the spiritual destitution of a
coral reef in the Pacific, or what it costs to look up the
precious souls among the cocoa-nuts and bread-fruit.

He goes to his crossing, and begins to lay it out for the
day. The town awakes; the great teetotum is set up for
its daily spin and whirl; all that unaccountable reading and

writing, which has been suspended for a few hours, recommences. Jo, and the other lower animals, get on in the unintelligible mess as they can. It is market-day. The blinded oxen, over-goaded, over-driven, never guided, run into wrong places and are beaten out; and plunge, red-eyed and foaming, at stone walls; and often sorely hurt the innocent, and often sorely hurt themselves. Very like Jo and his order; very, very like!

A band of music comes and plays. Jo listens to it. So does a dog—a drover's dog, waiting for his master outside a butcher's shop, and evidently thinking about those sheep he has had upon his mind for some hours, and is happily rid of. He seems perplexed respecting three or four; can't remember where he left them; looks up and down the street, as half expecting to see them astray; suddenly pricks up his ears and remembers all about it. A thoroughly vagabond dog, accustomed to low company and public-houses; a terrific dog to sheep; ready at a whistle to scamper over their backs, and tear out mouthfuls of their wool; but an educated, improved, developed dog, who has been taught his duties and knows how to discharge them. He and Jo listen to the music, probably with much the same amount of animal satisfaction; likewise, as to awakened association, aspiration or regret, melancholy or joyful reference to things beyond the senses, they are probably upon a par. But, otherwise, how far above the human listener is the brute!

Turn that dog's descendants wild, like Jo, and in a very few years they will so degenerate that they will lose even their bark—but not their bite.

The day changes as it wears itself away, and becomes dark and drizzly. Jo fights it out, at his crossing, among the mud and wheels, the horses, whips, and umbrellas, and gets but a scanty sum to pay for the unsavory shelter of Tom-all-Alone's. Twilight comes on; gas begins to start up in the shops; the lamplighter, with his ladder, runs along the margin of the pavement. A wretched evening is beginning to close in.

Inspector Bucket's Job

In his chambers, Mr. Tulkinghorn sits meditating an application to the nearest magistrate to-morrow morning for a warrant. Gridley, a disappointed suitor, has been here to-day, and has been alarming. We are not to be put in bodily fear, and that ill-conditioned fellow shall be held to bail again. From the ceiling, fore-shortened Allegory, in the person of one impossible Roman upside down, points with the arm of Samson (out of joint and an odd one) obtrusively towards the window. Why should Mr. Tulkinghorn, for no such reason, look out of window? Is the hand not always pointing there? So he does not look out of window.

And if he did, what would it be to see a woman going by? There are women enough in the world. Mr. Tulkinghorn thinks—too many; they are at the bottom of all that goes wrong in it, though, for the matter of that, they create business for lawyers. What would it be to see a woman going by, even though she were going secretly? They are all secret. Mr. Tulkinghorn knows that very well.

But they are not all like the woman who now leaves him and his house behind; between whose plain dress, and her refined manner, there is something exceedingly inconsistent. She should be an upper servant by her attire, yet, in her air and step, though both are hurried and assumed—as far as she can assume in the muddy streets, which she treads with an unaccustomed foot—she is a lady. Her face is veiled, and still she sufficiently betrays herself to make more than one of those who pass her look round sharply.

She never turns her head. Lady or servant, she has a purpose in her, and can follow it. She never turns her head, until she comes to the crossing where Jo plies with his broom. He crosses with her, and begs. Still, she does not turn her head until she has landed on the other side. Then, she slightly beckons to him, and says " Come here! "

Jo follows her, a pace or two, into a quiet court.

" Are you the boy I've read of in the papers? " she asked behind her veil.

"I don't know," says Jo, staring moodily at the veil, " nothink about no papers. I don't know nothink about nothink, at all."

"Were you examined at an inquest?"

"I don't know nothink about no—where I was took by the beadle, do you mean?" says Jo. "Was the boy's name at the inkwhich, Jo?"

"Yes."

"That's me!" says Jo.

"Come farther up."

"You mean about the man?" says Jo, following. "Him as wos dead?"

"Hush! Speak in a whisper! Yes. Did he look, when he was living, so very ill and poor?"

"O jist!" says Jo.

"Did he look like—not like *you?*" says the woman, with abhorrence.

"O not so bad as me," says Jo. "I'm a reg'lar one *I* am! You didn't know him, did you?"

"How dare you ask me if I knew him?"

"No offense, my lady," says Jo, with much humility; for even he has got at the suspicion of her being a lady.

"I am not a lady. I am a servant."

"You are a jolly servant!" says Jo; without the least idea of saying anything offensive; merely as a tribute of admiration.

"Listen and be silent. Don't talk to me, and stand farther from me! Can you show me all those places that were spoken of in the account I read? The place he wrote for, the place he died at, the place where you were taken to, the place where he was buried? Do you know the place where he was buried?"

Jo answers with a nod: having also nodded as each other place was mentioned.

"Go before me and show me all those dreadful places. Stop opposite to each, and don't speak to me unless I speak to you. Don't look back. Do what I want, and I will pay you well."

Jo attends closely while the words are being spoken; tells them off on his broom-handle, finding them rather hard; pauses to consider their meaning; considers it satisfactory, and nods his ragged head.

"I'm fly," says Jo. "But fen larks, you know. Stow hooking it!"

"What does the horrible creature mean?" exclaims the servant, recoiling from him.

"Stow cutting away, you know!" says Jo.

"I don't understand you. Go on before! I will give you more money than you ever had in your life."

Jo screws up his mouth into a whistle, gives his ragged head a rub, takes his broom under his arm, and leads the way; passing deftly, with his bare feet, over the hard stones, and through the mud and mire.

Cook's Court. Jo stops. A pause.

"Who lives here?"

"Him wot give him his writing, and give me half a bull," says Jo, in a whisper, without looking over his shoulder.

"Go on to the next!"

Krook's house. Jo stops again. A longer pause.

"Who lives here?"

"*He* lived here," Jo answers as before.

After a silence he is asked, "In which room?"

"In the back room up there. You can see the winder from this corner. Up there! That's where I see him stritched out. This is the public 'ouse where I was took to."

"Go on to the next!"

It was a longer walk to the next; but Jo, relieved of his first suspicions, sticks to the forms imposed upon him, and does not look round. By many devious ways, reeking with offense of many kinds, they come to the little tunnel of a court, and to the gas-lamp (lighted now), and to the iron gate.

"He was put there," says Jo, holding to the bars and looking in.

"Where? O, what a scene of horror!"

"There!" says Jo, pointing. "Over yinder. Among them piles of bones, and close to that there kitchin winder! They put him wery nigh the top. They was obliged to stamp upon it to get it in. I could unkiver it for you with my broom, if the gate was open. That's why they locks it, I s'pose," giving it a shake. "It's always locked. Look at the rat!" cries Jo, excited. "Hi! Look! There he goes! Ho! Into the ground!"

The servant shrinks into a corner—into a corner of that hideous archway, with its deadly stains contaminating her dress; and putting out her two hands, and passionately telling him to keep away from her, for he is loathsome to her, so remains for some moments. Jo stands staring, and is still staring when she recovers herself.

"Is this place of abomination consecrated ground?"

"I don't know nothink of consequential ground," says Jo, still staring.

"Is it blessed?"

"Which?" says Jo, in the last degree amazed.

"Is it blessed?"

"I'm blest if I know," says Jo, staring more than ever; "but I shouldn't think it warn't. Blest?" repeats Jo, something troubled in his mind. "It ain't done it much good if it is. Blest? I should think it was t'othered myself. But I don't know nothink!"

The servant takes as little heed of what he says, as she seems to take of what she has said herself. She draws off her glove, to get some money from her purse. Jo silently notices how white and small her hand is, and what a jolly servant she must be to wear such sparkling rings.

She drops a piece of money in his hand, without touching it, and shuddering as their hands approach. "Now," she adds, "show me the spot again!"

Jo thrusts the handle of his broom between the bars of the gate, and, with his utmost power of elaboration, points it out. At length, looking aside to see if he has made himself intelligible, he finds that he is alone.

His first proceeding, is, to hold the piece of money to

the gas-light, and to be overpowered at finding that it is yellow—gold. His next, is, to give it a one-sided bite at the edge, as a test of its quality. His next, to put it in his mouth for safety, and to sweep the step and passage with great care. His job done, he sets off for Tom-all-Alone's; stopping in the light of innumerable gas-lamps to produce the piece of gold, and give it another one-sided bite, as a reassurance of its being genuine.

The Mercury in powder is in no want of society to-night, for my Lady goes to a grand dinner, and three or four balls. Sir Leicester is fidgety, down at Chesney Wold, with no better company than the gout; he complains to Mrs. Rouncewell that the rain makes such a monotonous pattering on the terrace, that he can't read the paper, even by the fireside in his own snug dressing-room.

"Sir Leicester would have done better to try the other side of the house, my dear," says Mrs. Rouncewell to Rosa. "His dressing-room is on my Lady's side. And in all these years I never heard the step upon the Ghost's Walk, more distinct than it is to-night!"

VII

MOVING ON.

It is the long vacation in the regions of Chancery Lane. The good ships Law and Equity, those teak-built, copper-bottomed, iron-fastened, brazen-faced, and not by any means fast-sailing Clippers, are laid up in ordinary. The Flying Dutchman, with a crew of ghostly clients imploring all whom they may encounter to peruse their papers, has drifted, for the time being, Heaven knows where. The Courts are all shut up; the public offices lie in a hot sleep; Westminster Hall itself is a shady solitude where night-ingales might sing, and a tenderer class of suitors than is usually found there, walk.

The Temple, Chancery Lane, Serjeants' Inn, and Lincoln's Inn even unto the Fields, are like tidal harbors at low water; where stranded proceedings, offices at anchor, idle clerks lounging on lop-sided stools that will not recover their perpendicular until the current of Term sets in, lie high and dry upon the ooze of the long vacation. Outer doors of chambers are shut up by the score, messages and parcels are to be left at the Porter's Lodge by the bushel. A crop of grass would grow in the chinks of the stone pavement outside Lincoln's Inn Hall, but that the ticket-porters, who have nothing to do beyond sitting in the shade there, with their white aprons over their heads to keep the flies off, grub it up and eat it thoughtfully.

There is only one Judge in town. Even he only comes twice a-week to sit in chambers. If the country folks of those assize towns on his circuit could see him now! No full-bottomed wig, no red petticoats, no fur, no javelin-men, no white wands. Merely a close-shaved gentleman in white trousers and a white hat, with sea-bronze on the judicial countenance, and a strip of bark peeled by the solar rays from the judicial nose, who calls in at the shell-fish shop as he comes along, and drinks iced ginger-beer!

The bar of England is scattered over the face of the earth. How England can get on through four long summer months without its bar—which is its acknowledged refuge in adversity, and its only legitimate triumph in prosperity—is beside the question; assuredly that shield and buckler of Britannia are not in present wear. The learned gentleman who is always so tremendously indignant at the unprecedented outrage committed on the feelings of his client by the opposite party, that he never seems likely to recover it, is doing infinitely better than might be expected, in Switzerland. The learned gentleman who does the withering business, and who blights all opponents with his gloomy sarcasm, is as merry as a grig at a French watering-place. The learned gentleman who weeps by the pint on the smallest provocation, has not shed a tear these six weeks. The very learned gentleman who has cooled the national heat of his gingery complexion in pools and fountains of law, until he has become great in knotty arguments for term-time, when he poses the drowsy Bench with legal "chaff," inexplicable to the uninitiated and to most of the initiated too, is roaming, with a characteristic delight in aridity and dust, about Constantinople. Other dispersed fragments of the same great Palladium are to be found on the canals of Venice, at the second cataract of the Nile, in the baths of Germany, and sprinkled on the sea-sand all over the English coast. Scarcely one is to be encountered in the deserted region of Chancery Lane. If such a lonely member of the bar do flit across the waste, and come upon a prowling suitor who is unable to leave off haunting the scenes of his anxiety, they frighten one another, and retreat into opposite shades.

It is the hottest long vacation known for many years. All the young clerks are madly in love, and, according to their various degrees, pine for bliss with the beloved object, at Margate, Ramsgate, or Gravesend. All the middle-aged clerks think their family too large. All the unowned dogs who stray into the Inns of Court, and pant about staircases and other dry places, seeking water, give short howls of aggravation. All the blind men's dogs in the streets draw their masters against pumps, or trip them over buckets. A shop with a sun-blind, and a watered pavement, and a bowl of gold and silver fish in the window, is a sanctuary. Temple Bar gets so hot, that it is, to the adjacent Strand and Fleet Street, what a heater is in an urn, and keeps them simmering all night.

There are offices about the Inns of Court in which a man might be cool, if any coolness were worth purchasing at such a price in dulness; but, the little thoroughfares immediately outside those retirements seem to blaze. In Mr. Krook's court it is so hot that the people turn their houses inside out, and sit in chairs upon the pavement—Mr. Krook included, who there pursues his studies, with his cat (who never is too hot), by his side. The Sol's Arms has discontinued the harmonic meetings for the season, and Little Swills is engaged at the Pastoral Gardens down the river, where he comes out in quite an innocent manner, and sings comic ditties of a juvenile complexion, calculated (as the bill says) not to wound the feelings of the most fastidious mind.

Over all the legal neighborhood, there hangs, like some great veil of rust, or gigantic cobweb, the idleness and pensiveness of the long vacation. Mr. Snagsby, law-stationer of Cook's Court, Cursitor Street, is sensible of the influence; not only in his mind as a sympathetic and contemplative man, but also in his business as a law-stationer aforesaid. He has more leisure for musing in Staple Inn and in the Rolls Yard, during the long vacation, than at other seasons; and he says to the two 'prentices, what a thing it is in such hot weather to think that you live in an island, with the sea a-rolling and a-bowling right round you.

Guster is busy in the little drawing-room, on this present afternoon in the long vacation, when Mr. and Mrs. Snagsby have it in contemplation to receive company. The expected guests are rather select than numerous, being Mr. and Mrs. Chadband, and no more. From Mr. Chadband's being much given to describe himself, both verbally and in writing, as a vessel, he is occasionally mistaken by strangers for a gentleman connected with navigation; but, he is, as he expresses it, "in the ministry." Mr. Chadband is attached to no particular denomination; and is considered by his persecutors to have nothing so very remarkable to say on the greatest of subjects as to render his volunteering, on his own account, at all incumbent on his conscience; but, he has his followers, and Mrs. Snagsby is of the number. Mrs. Snagsby has but recently taken a passage upward by the vessel, Chadband; and her attention was attracted to that Bark A1, when she was something flushed by the hot weather.

"My little woman," says Mr. Snagsby to the sparrows in Staple Inn, "likes to have her religion rather sharp, you see!"

So, Guster, much impressed by regarding herself for the time as the handmaid of Chadband, whom she knows to be endowed with the gift of holding forth for four hours at a stretch, prepares the little drawing-room for tea. All the furniture is shaken and dusted, the portraits of Mr. and Mrs. Snagsby are touched up with a wet cloth, the best tea-service is set forth, and there is excellent provision made of dainty new bread, crusty twists, cool fresh butter, thin slices of ham, tongue, and German sausage, and delicate little rows of anchovies nestling in parsley; not to mention new-laid eggs, to be brought up warm in a napkin, and hot buttered toast. For, Chadband is rather a consuming vessel—the persecutors say a gorging vessel; and can wield such weapons of the flesh as a knife and fork, remarkably well.

Mr. Snagsby in his best coat, looking at all the preparations when they are completed, and coughing his cough of deference behind his hand, says to Mrs. Snagsby, " At what time did you expect Mr. and Mrs. Chadband, my love? "

" At six," says Mrs. Snagsby.

Mr. Snagsby observes in a mild and casual way, that " it's gone that."

" Perhaps you'd like to begin without them," is Mrs. Snagsby's reproachful remark.

Mr. Snagsby does look as if he would like it very much, but he says, with his cough of mildness, " No, my dear, no, I merely named the time."

" What's time," says Mrs. Snagsby, " to eternity? "

" Very true my dear," says Mr. Snagsby. " Only when a person lays in victuals for tea, a person does it with a view—perhaps—more to time. And when a time is named for having tea, it's better to come up to it."

" To come up to it! " Mrs. Snagsby repeats the severity. " Up to it! As if Mr. Chadband was a fighter! "

" Not at all, my dear," says Mr. Snagsby.

Here, Guster, who had been looking out of the bedroom window, comes rustling and scratching down the little staircase like a popular ghost, and, falling flushed into the drawing-room, announces that Mr. and Mrs. Chadband have appeared in the court. The bell at the inner door in the passage immediately thereafter tinkling, she is admonished by Mrs. Snagsby, on pain of instant reconsignment to her patron saint, not to omit the ceremony of announcement. Much discomposed in her nerves (which were previously in the best order) by this threat, she so fearfully mutilates that point of state as to announce " Mr. and Mrs. Cheeseming, least which, Imeantersay, whatesername!" and retires conscience-stricken, from the presence.

Mr. Chadband is a large yellow man, with a fat smile, and a general appearance of having a good deal of train oil in his system. Mrs. Chadband is a stern, severe-looking, silent woman. Mr. Chadband moves softly and cumbrously, not unlike a bear who has been taught to walk upright. He is very much embarrassed about the arms, as if they were inconvenient to him, and he wanted to grovel; is very much in a perspiration about the head; and never speaks without first putting up his great hand, as delivering a token to his hearers that he is going to edify them.

" My friends," said Mr. Chadband, " Peace be on this house! On the master thereof, on the mistress thereof, on the young maidens, and on the young men! My friends, why do I wish for peace? What is peace? Is it war? No. Is it strife? No. Is it lovely, and gentle, and beautiful, and pleasant, and serene, and joyful? O yes! Therefore, my friends, I wish for peace, upon you and upon yours."

In consequence of Mrs. Snagsby looking deeply edified, Mr. Snagsby thinks it expedient on the whole to say Amen, which is well received.

" Now, my friends," proceeds Mr. Chadband, " since I am upon this theme——"

Guster presents herself. Mrs. Snagsby, in a spectral bass voice, and without removing her eyes from Chadband, says, with dread distinctness, " Go away?"

" Now, my friends," says Chadband, " since I am upon this theme, and in my lowly path improving it——"

Guster is heard unaccountably to murmur " one thousing seven hundred and eighty-two." The spectral voice repeats more solemnly, " Go away!"

" Now, my friends," says Mr. Chadband, " we will inquire in a spirit of love——"

Still Guster reiterates " one thousing seven hundred and eighty-two."

Mr. Chadband, pausing with the resignation of a man accustomed to be persecuted, and languidly folding up his chin into his fat smile, says, " Let us hear the maiden! Speak, maiden! "

" One thousing seven hundred and eighty-two, if you please, sir. Which he wish to know what the shilling ware for," says Guster, breathless.

" For? " returns Mrs. Chadband. " For his fare! "

Guster replied that " he insists on one and eightpence, or on summonsizzing the party." Mrs. Snagsby and Mrs. Chadband are proceeding to grow shrill in indignation, when Mr. Chadband quiets the tumult by lifting up his hand.

" My friends," says he, " I remember a duty unfulfilled yesterday. It is right that I should be chastened in some penalty. I ought not to murmur. Rachael, pay the eightpence! "

While Mrs. Snagsby, drawing her breath, looks hard at Mr. Snagsby, as who should say, " You hear this Apostle! " and while Mr. Chadband glows with humidity and train oil, Mrs. Chadband pays the money. It is Mr. Chadband's habit—it is the head and front of his pretensions indeed—to keep this sort of debtor and creditor account in the smallest items, and to post it publicly on the most trivial occasions.

" My friends," says Chadband, " eightpence is not much; it might justly have been one and fourpence; it might justly have been half-a-crown. O let us be joyful, joyful! O let us be joyful! "

With which remark, which appears from its sound to be an extract in verse, Mr. Chadband stalks to the table, and, before taking a chair, lifts up his admonitory hand.

" My friends," says he, " what is this which we now behold as being spread before us? Refreshment. Do we need refreshment, then, my friends? We do. And why do we need refreshment, my friends? Because we are but mortal, because we are but sinful, because we are but of earth, because we are not of the air. Can we fly, my friends? We cannot. Why can we not fly, my friends?"

Mr. Snagsby, presuming on the success of his last point, ventures to observe in a cheerful and rather knowing tone, "No wings." But, is immediately frowned down by Mrs. Snagsby.

"I say, my friends," pursues Mr. Chadband, utterly rejecting and obliterating Mr. Snagsby's suggestion, "why can we not fly? Is it because we are calculated to walk? It is. Could we walk, my friends, without strength? We could not. What should we do without strength, my friends? Our legs would refuse to bear us, our knees would double up, our ankles would turn over, and we should come to the ground. Then from whence, my friends, in a human point of view, do we derive the strength that is necessary to our limbs? Is it," says Chadband, glancing over the table, "from bread in various forms, from butter which is churned from the milk which is yielded unto us by the cow, from the eggs which are laid by the fowl, from ham, from tongue, from sausage, and from such like? It is. Then let us partake of the good things which are set before us!"

The persecutors denied that there was any particular gift in Mr. Chadband's piling verbose flights of stairs, one upon another, after this fashion. But this can only be received as a proof of their determination to persecute, since it must be within everybody's experience, that the Chadband style of oratory is widely received and much admired.

Mr. Chadband, however, having concluded for the present, sits down at Mr. Snagsby's table, and lays about him prodigiously. The conversion of nutriment of any sort into oil of the quality already mentioned, appears to be a process so inseparable from the constitution of this exemplary vessel, that in beginning to eat and drink, he may be described as always becoming a kind of considerable Oil Mills or other large factory for the production of that ar-

ticle on a wholesale scale. On the present evening of the
long vacation, in Cook's Court, Cursitor Street, he does
such a powerful stroke of business, that the warehouse
appears to be quite full when the work ceases.

At this period of the entertainment, Guster, who has
never recovered her first failure, but has neglected no
possible or impossible means of bringing the establishment
and herself into contempt—among which may be briefly
enumerated her unexpectedly performing clashing military
music on Mr. Chadband's head with plates, and afterwards
crowning that gentleman with muffins—at which period of
the entertainment, Guster whispers Mr. Snagsby that he is
wanted.

" And being wanted in the—not to put too fine a point
upon it—in the shop! " says Mr. Snagsby rising, " perhaps
this good company will excuse me for half a minute."

Mr. Snagsby descends, and finds the two 'prentices intently contemplating a police constable, who holds a ragged
boy by the arm.

" Why, bless my heart," says Mr. Snagsby, " what's the
matter?"

" This boy," says the constable, " although he's repeatedly
told to, won't move on——"

" I'm always a-moving on, sir," cries the boy, wiping
away his grimy tears with his arm. " I've always been
a-moving and a-moving on, ever since I was born. Where
can I possibly move to, sir, more nor I do move! "

" He won't move on," says the constable, calmly, with a
slight professional hitch of his neck involving its better
settlement in his stiff stock, " although he has been repeatedly cautioned, and therefore I am obliged to take him into
custody. He's as obstinate a young gonoph as I know.
He won't move on."

" O my eye! Where can I move to?" cries the boy,
clutching quite desperately at his hair, and beating his bare
feet upon the floor of Mr. Snagsby's passage.

" Don't you come none of that, or I shall make blessed
short work of you! " says the constable, giving him a pas-

sionless shake. " My instructions are, that you are to move on. I have told you so five hundred times."

" But where? " cries the boy.

" Well! Really, constable, you know," says Mr. Snagsby, wistfully, and coughing behind his hand his cough of great perplexity and doubt; " really that does seem a question. Where, you know? "

" My instructions don't go to that," replies the constable. " My instructions are that this boy is to move on."

Do you hear, Jo? It is nothing to you, or to anyone else, that the great lights of the parliamentary sky have failed for some few years, in this business, to set you the example of moving on. The one grand recipe remains for you—the profound philosophical prescription—the be-all and the end-all of your strange existence upon earth. Move on! You are by no means to move off, Jo, for the great lights can't at all agree about that. Move on!

Mr. Snagsby says nothing to this effect; says nothing at all, indeed; but coughs his forlornest cough, expressive of no thoroughfare in any direction. By this time Mr. and Mrs. Chadband, and Mrs. Snagsby, hearing the altercation, have appeared upon the stairs. Guster having never left the end of the passage, the whole household are assembled.

" The simple question is, sir," says the constable, " whether you know this boy. He says you do."

Mrs. Snagsby, from her elevation, instantly cries out, " No, he don't! "

" My little woman! " says Mr. Snagsby, looking up the staircase. " My love, permit me! Pray have a moment's patience, my dear. I do know something of this lad, and in what I know of him, I can't say that there's any harm; perhaps on the contrary, constable." To whom the law-stationer relates his Joful and woful experience, suppressing the half-crown fact.

" Well! " says the constable, " so far, it seems, he had grounds for what he said. When I took him into custody up in Holborn, he said you knew him. Upon that, a young man who was in the crowd said he was acquainted with you, and you were a respectable housekeeper, and if I'd call and make the inquiry, he'd appear. The young man don't seem inclined to keep his word, but—Oh! Here *is* the young man!"

Enter Mr. Guppy, who nods to Mr. Snagsby, and touches his hat with the chivalry of clerkship to the ladies on the stairs.

"I was strolling away from the office just now, when I found this row going on," says Mr. Guppy to the law-stationer; "and as your name was mentioned, I thought it was right the thing should be looked into."

"It was very good-natured of you, sir," says Mr. Snagsby, "and I am obliged to you." And Mr. Snagsby again relates his experience, again suppressing the half-crown fact.

"Now, I know where you live," says the constable, then, to Jo. "You live down in Tom-all-Alone's. That's a nice innocent place to live in, ain't it?"

"I can't go and live in no nicer place, sir," replies Jo. "They wouldn't have nothink to say to me if I wos to go to a nice innocent place fur to live. Who ud go and let a nice innocent lodging to such a reg'lar one as me?"

"You are very poor, ain't you?" says the constable.

"Yes, I am indeed, sir, wery poor in gin'ral," replies Jo.

"I leave you to judge now! I shook these two half-crowns out of him," says the constable, producing them to the company, "in only putting my hand upon him!"

"They're wot's left, Mr. Snagsby," says Jo, "out of a sov'ring as wos give me by a lady in a wale as sed she wos a servant and as come to my crossin one night and asked to be showed this 'ere ouse and the ouse wot him as you giv the writin to died at, and the berrin-ground wot he's berrid in. She ses to me she ses 'are you the boy at Ink-which?' she ses. I ses 'yes' I ses. She ses to me she ses 'can you show me all them places?' I ses 'yes I can' I ses. And she ses to me 'do it' and I dun it and she giv me a sov'ring and hooked it. And I ain't had much of the sov'ring neither," says Jo, with dirty tears,

" fur I had to pay five bob, down in Tom-all-Alone's, afore they'd square it fur to give me change, and then a young man he thieved another five while I was asleep and another boy he thieved ninepence and the landlord he stood drains round with a lot more on it."

" You don't expect anybody to believe this, about the lady and the sovereign, do you?" says the constable, eying him aside with ineffable disdain.

" I don't know as I do, sir," replies Jo. " I don't expect nothink at all, sir, much, but that's the true hist'ry on it."

" You see what he is!" the constable observes to the audience. " Well, Mr, Snagsby, if I don't lock him up this time, will you engage for his moving on?"

" No!" cries Mrs. Snagsby from the stairs.

" My little woman!" pleads her husband. " Constable, I have no doubt he'll move on. You know you really must do it," says Mr. Snagsby.

" I'm everyways agreeable, sir," says the hapless Jo.

" Do it, then," observes the constable, " You know what you have got to do. Do it! And recollect you won't get off so easy next time. Catch hold of your money. Now, the sooner you're five mile off, the better for all parties."

With this farewell hint, and pointing generally to the setting sun, as a likely place to move on to, the constable bids his auditors good afternoon; and makes the echoes of Cook's Court perform slow music for him as he walks away on the shady side, carrying his iron-bound hat in his hand for a little ventilation.

Now, Jo's improbable story concerning the lady and the sovereign has awakened more or less the curiosity of all the company. Mr. Guppy, who has an inquiring mind in matters of evidence, and who has been suffering severely from the lassitude of the long vacation, takes that interest in the case, that he enters on a regular cross-examination of the witness, which is found so interesting by the ladies that Mrs. Snagsby politely invites him to step upstairs, and drink a cup of tea, if he will excuse the disarranged state of the tea-table, consequent on their previous exertions.

Mr. Guppy yielding his assent to this proposal, Jo is requested to follow into the drawing-room doorway, where Mr. Guppy takes him in hand as a witness, patting him into this shape, that shape, and the other shape, like a butterman dealing with so much butter, and worrying him according to the best models. Nor is the examination unlike many such model displays, both in respect of its eliciting nothing and of its being lengthy; for, Mr. Guppy is sensible of his talent, and Mrs. Snagsby feels, not only that it gratifies her inquisitive disposition, but that it lifts her husband's establishment higher up in the law. During the progress of this keen encounter, the vessel Chadband, being merely engaged in the oil trade, gets aground, and waits to be floated off.

"Well!" says Mr. Guppy, "either this boy sticks to it like cobbler's-wax, or there is something out of the common here that beats anything that ever came into my way at Kenge and Carboy's."

Mr. Chadband, at last seeing his opportunity, makes his accustomed signal, and rises with a smoking head, which he dabs with his pocket-handkerchief. Mrs. Snagsby whispers "Hush!"

"My friends," says Chadband, "we have partaken in moderation" (which was certainly not the case so far as he was concerned), "of the comforts which have been provided for us. May this house live upon the fatness of the land; may corn and wine be plentiful therein; may it grow, may it thrive, may it prosper, may it advance, may it proceed, may it press forward! But, my friends, have we partaken of anything else? We have. My friends, of what else have we partaken? Of spiritual profit? From whence have we derived that spiritual profit? My young friend, stand forth!"

Jo, thus apostrophized, gives a slouch backward, and another slouch forward, and another slouch to each side, and confronts the eloquent Chadband, with evident doubts of his intentions.

"My young friend," says Chadband, "you are to us a

pearl, you are to us a diamond, you are to us a gem, you are to us a jewel. And why, my young friend?"

"I don't know," replies Jo. "I don't know nothink."

"My young friend," says Chadband, "it is because you know nothing that you are to us a gem and jewel. For what are you, my young friend? Are you a beast of the field? No. A bird of the air? No. A fish of the sea or river? No. You are a human boy, my young friend. A human boy. O glorious to be a human boy! And why glorious, my young friend? Because you are capable of receiving the lessons of wisdom, because you are capable of profiting by this discourse which I now deliver for your good, because you are not a stick, or a staff, or a stock, or a stone, or a post, or a pillar.

> "'O running stream of sparkling joy,
>   To be a soaring human boy!'

And do you cool yourself in that stream now, my young friend? No. Why do you not cool yourself in that stream now? Because you are in a state of darkness, because you are in a state of obscurity, because you are in a state of sinfulness, because you are in a state of bondage. My young friend, what *is* bondage? Let us, in a spirit of love, inquire."

At this threatening stage of the discourse, Jo, who seems to have been gradually going out of his mind, smears his right arm over his face, and gives a terrible yawn. Mrs. Snagsby indignantly expresses her belief that he is a limb of the arch-fiend.

"My friends," says Mr. Chadband, with his persecuted chin folding itself into its fat smile again as he looks round, "it is right that I should be humbled, it is right that I should be tried, it is right that I should be mortified, it is right that I should be corrected. I stumbled, on Sabbath last, when I thought with pride of my three hours' improving. The account is now favorably balanced; my creditor has accepted a composition. O let us be joyful, joyful! O let us be joyful!"

Great sensation on the part of Mrs. Snagsby.

"My friends," says Chadband, looking round him in conclusion. "I will not proceed with my young friend now. Will you come to-morrow, my young friend, and inquire of this good lady where I am to be found to deliver a discourse unto you, and will you come like the thirsty swallow upon the next day, and upon the day after that, and upon the day after that, and upon many pleasant days, to hear discourses?" (This with a cow-like lightness.)

Jo, whose immediate object seems to be to get away on any terms, gives a shuffling nod. Mr. Guppy then throws him a penny, and Mrs. Snagsby calls to Guster to see him safely out of the house. But, before he goes downstairs, Mr. Snagsby loads him with some broken meats from the table, which he carries away, hugging in his arms.

So, Mr. Chadband—of whom the persecutors say that it is no wonder he should go on for any length of time uttering such abominable nonsense, but that the wonder rather is that he should ever leave off, having once the audacity to begin—retires into private life until he invests a little capital of supper in the oil-trade. Jo moves on, through the long vacation, down to Blackfrairs Bridge, where he finds a baking stony corner, wherein to settle to his repast.

And there he sits, munching and gnawing, and looking up at the great Cross on the summit of St. Paul's Cathedral, glittering above a red and violet-tinted cloud of smoke. From the boy's face one might suppose that sacred emblem to be, in his eyes, the crowning confusion of the great, confused city; so golden, so high up, so far out of his reach. There he sits, the sun going down, the river running fast, the crowd flowing by him in two streams— everything moving on to some purpose and to one end— until he is stirred up, and told to "move on" too.

VIII

MR. BUCKET

ALLEGORY looks pretty cool in Lincoln's Inn Fields, though the evening is hot; for, both Mr. Tulkinghorn's windows are wide open, and the room is lofty, gusty, and gloomy. These may not be desirable characteristics when November comes with fog and sleet, or January with ice and snow; but they have their merits in the sultry long vacation weather. They enable Allegory, though it has cheeks like peaches, and knees like bunches of blossoms, and rosy swellings for calves to its legs and muscles to its arms, to look tolerably cool to-night.

Plenty of dust comes in at Mr. Tulkinghorn's windows, and plenty more has generated among his furniture and papers. It lies thick everywhere. When a breeze from the country. that has lost its way, takes fright, and makes a blind hurry to rush out again, it flings as much dust in the eyes of Allegory as the law—or Mr. Tulkinghorn, one of its trustiest representatives—may scatter, on occasion, in the eyes of the laity.

In his towering magazine of dust, the universal article into which his papers and himself, and all his clients, and all things of earth, animate and inanimate, are resolving, Mr. Tulkinghorn sits at one of the open windows, enjoying a bottle of old port. Though a hard-grained man, close, dry, and silent, he can enjoy old wine with the best. He has a priceless binn of port in some artful cellar under the Fields, which is one of his many secrets. When he dines alone in chambers, as he has dined to-day, and has his bit of fish and his steak or chicken brought in from the coffee-house, he descends with a candle to the echoing regions below the deserted mansion, and, heralded by a remote reverberation of thundering doors, comes gravely back, encircled by an earthly atmosphere, and carrying a bottle from which he pours a radiant nectar, two score and ten years

79

old, that blushes in the glass to find itself so famous, and fills the whole room with the fragrance of southern grapes.

Mr. Tulkinghorn, sitting in the twilight by the open window, enjoys his wine. As if it whispered to him of its fifty years of silence and seclusion, it shuts him up the closer. More impenetrable than ever, he sits and drinks, and mellows, as it were, in secrecy; pondering, at that twilight hour, on all the mysteries he knows, associated with darkening woods in the country, and vast blank shut-up houses in town; and perhaps sparing a thought or two for himself, and his family history, and his money, and his will—all a mystery to everyone—and that one bachelor friend of his, a man of the same mould and a lawyer, too, who lived the same kind of life until he was seventy-five years old, and then, suddenly conceiving (as it is supposed) an impression that it was too monotonous, gave his gold watch to his hair dresser one summer evening, and walked leisurely home to the Temple, and hanged himself.

But, Mr. Tulkinghorn is not alone to-night, to ponder at his usual length. Seated at the same table, though with his chair modestly and uncomfortably drawn a little way from it, sits a bald, mild, shining man, who coughs respectfully behind his hand when the lawyer bids him fill his glass.

" Now, Snagsby," says Mr. Tulkinghorn, " to go over this odd story again."

" If you please, sir."

" You told me when you were so good as to step round here, last night——"

" For which I must ask you to excuse me if it was a liberty, sir; but I remember that you had taken a sort of an interest in that person, and I thought it possible that you might—just—wish—to——"

Mr. Tulkinghorn is not the man to help him to any conclusion, or to admit anything as to any possibility concerning himself. So Mr. Snagsby trails off into saying, with an awkward cough, " I must ask you to excuse the liberty, sir, I am sure."

"Not at all," says Mr. Tulkinghorn. "You told me, Snagsby, that you put on your hat and came round without mentioning your intention to your wife. That was prudent, I think, because it's not a matter of such importance that it requires to be mentioned."

"Well, sir," returns Mr. Snagsby, "you see my little woman is—not to put too fine a point upon it—inquisitive. She's inquisitive. Poor little thing, she's liable to spasms, and it's good for her to have her mind employed. In consequence of which she employs it—I should say upon every individual thing she can lay hold of, whether it concerns her or not—especially not. My little women has a very active mind, sir."

Mr. Snagsby drinks, and murmurs with an admiring cough behind his hand, "Dear me, very fine wine, indeed!"

"Therefore you kept your visit to yourself, last night?" says Mr. Tulkinghorn. "And to-night, too?"

"Yes, sir, and to-night, too. My little woman is at present in—not to put too fine a point on it—in a pious state, or in what she considers such, and attends the Evening Exertions (which is the name they go by) of a reverend party of the name of Chadband. He has a great deal of eloquence at his command, undoubtedly, but I am not quite favorable to his style myself. That's neither here nor there. My little woman being engaged in that way, made it easier for me to step round in a quiet manner."

Mr. Tulkinghorn assents. "Fill your glass, Snagsby."

"Thank you, sir, I am sure," returns the stationer, with his cough of deference. "This is wonderfully fine wine, sir!"

"It is a rare wine now," says Mr. Tulkinghorn. "It is fifty years old."

"Is it indeed, sir? But I am not surprised to hear it, I am sure. It might be—any age almost." After rendering this general tribute to the port, Mr. Snagsby in his modesty coughs an apology behind his hand for drinking anything so precious.

"Will you run over, once again, what the boy said?" asks Mr. Tulkinghorn, putting his hands into the pockets of his rusty smallclothes and leaning quietly back in his chair.

"With pleasure, sir."

Then, with fidelity, though with some prolixity, the law-stationer repeats Jo's statement made to the assembled guests at his house. On coming to the end of his narrative, he gives a great start, and breaks off with—"Dear me, sir, I wasn't aware there was any other gentleman present!"

Mr. Snagsby is dismayed to see, standing with an attentive face between himself and the lawyer, at a little distance from the table, a person with a hat and stick in his hand, who was not there when he himself came in, and has not since entered by the door or by either of the windows. There is a press in the room, but its hinges have not creaked, nor has a step been audible upon the floor. Yet this third person stands there, with his attentive face, and his hat and stick in his hands, and his hands behind him, a composed and quiet listener. He is a stoutly built, steady-looking, sharp-eye man in black, of about the middle-age. Except that he looks at Mr. Snagsby as if he were going to take his portrait, there is nothing remarkable about him at first sight but his ghostly manner of appearing.

"Don't mind this gentleman," says Mr. Tulkinghorn, in his quiet way. "This is only Mr. Bucket."

"O indeed, sir?" returns the stationer, expressing by a cough that he is quite in the dark as to who Mr. Bucket may be.

"I wanted him to hear this story," say the lawyer, "because I have half a mind (for a reason) to know more of it, and he is very intelligent in such things. What do you say to this, Bucket?"

"It's very plain, sir. Since our people have moved this boy on, and he's not to be found on his old lay, if Mr. Snagsby don't object to go down with me to Tom-all-Alone's and point him out, we can have him here in less than a couple of hours' time. I can do it without Mr. Snagsby, of course; but this is the shortest way."

"Mr. Bucket is a detective officer, Snagsby," says the lawyer in explanation.

"Is he, indeed, sir?" says Mr. Snagsby, with a strong tendency in his clump of hair to stand on end.

"And if you have no real objection to accompany Mr. Bucket to the place in question," pursues the lawyer, "I shall feel obliged to you if you will do so."

In a moment's hesitation on the part of Mr. Snagsby, Bucket dips down to the bottom of his mind.

"Don't you be afraid of hurting the boy," he says. "You won't do that. It's all right as far as the boy's concerned. We shall only bring him here to ask him a question or so I want to put to him, and he'll be paid for his trouble, and sent away again. It'll be a good job for him. I promise you, as a man, that you shall see the boy sent away all right. Don't you be afraid of hurting him; you ain't going to do that."

"Very well, Mr. Tulkinghorn!" cries Mr. Snagsby cheerfully, and reassured, "since that's the case——"

"Yes! and lookee here, Mr. Snagsby," resumes Bucket, taking him aside by the arm, tapping him familiarly on the breast, and speaking in a confidential tone. "You're a man of the world, you know, and a man of business, and a man of sense. That's what *you* are."

"I am sure I am much obliged to you for your good opinion," returns the stationer, with his cough of modesty, "but——"

"That's what *you* are, you know," says Bucket. "Now, it ain't necessary to say to a man like you, engaged in your business, which is a business of trust and requires a person to be wide awake and have his senses about him, and his head screwed on tight (I had an uncle in your business once)—it ain't necessary to say to a man like you, that it's the best and wisest way to keep little matters like this quiet. Don't you see? Quiet!"

"Certainly, certainly," returns the other.

Inspector Bucket's Job

"I don't mind telling *you*," says Bucket, with an engaging appearance of frankness, "that as far as I can understand it, there seems to be a doubt whether this dead person wasn't entitled to a little property, and whether this female hasn't been up to some games respecting that property, don't you see?"

"O!" says Mr. Snagsby, but not appearing to see quite distinctly.

"Now, what *you* want," pursues Bucket, again, tapping Mr. Snagsby on the breast in a comfortable and soothing manner, "is, that every person should have their rights according to justice. That's what *you* want."

"To be sure," returns Mr. Snagsby, with a nod.

"On account of which, and at the same time to oblige a— do you call it, in your business, customer or client? I forget how my uncle used to call it."

"Why, I generally say customer myself," replies Mr. Snagsby.

"You're right!" returns Mr. Bucket, shaking hands with him quite affectionately,—"on account of which, and at the same time to oblige a real good customer, you mean to go down with me, in confidence, to Tom-all-Alone's, and to keep the whole thing quiet ever afterwards and never mention it to anyone. That's about your intentions, if I understand you?"

"You are right, sir. You are right," says Mr. Snagsby.

"Then here's your hat," returns his new friend, quite as intimate with it as if he had made it; "and if you're ready, I am."

They leave Mr. Tulkinghorn, without a ruffle on the surface of his unfathomable depths, drinking his old wine, and go down into the streets.

"You don't happen to know a very good sort of person of the name of Gridley, do you?" says Bucket, in a friendly converse as they descended the stairs.

"No," says Mr. Snagsby, considering, "I don't know anybody of that name. Why?"

"Nothing particular," says Bucket; "only, having al-

84

lowed his temper to get a trifle the better of him, and having been threatening some respectable people, he is keeping out of the way of a warrant I have got against him—which it's a pity that a man of sense should do."

As they walk along, Mr. Snagsby observes, as a novelty, that, however quick their pace may be, his companion still seems in some undefinable manner to lurk and lounge; also, that whenever he is going to turn to the right or left, he pretends to have a fixed purpose in his mind of going straight ahead, and wheels off, sharply, at the very last moment. Now and then, when they pass a police-constable on his beat, Mr. Snagsby notices that both the constable and his guide fall into a deep abstraction as they come towards each other, and appear entirely to overlook each other, and to gaze into space. In a few instances, Mr. Bucket coming behind some under-sized young man with a shining hat on, and his sleek hair twisted into one flat curl on each side of his head, almost without glancing at him touches him with his stick; upon which the young man, looking round, instantly evaporates. For the most part Mr. Bucket notices things in general, with a face as unchanging as the great mourning ring on his little finger, or the brooch, composed of not much diamond and a good deal of setting, which he wears in his shirt.

When they come at last to Tom-all-Alone's, Mr. Bucket stops for a moment at the corner, and takes a lighted bull's-eye from the constable on duty there, who then accompanies him with his own particular bull's-eye at his waist. Between his two conductors, Mr. Snagsby passes along the middle of a villainous street, undrained, unventilated, deep in black mud and corrupt water—though the roads are dry elsewhere—and reeking with such smells and sights that he, who has lived in London all his life, can scarce believe his senses. Branching from this street and its heaps of ruins, are other streets and courts so infamous that Mr. Snagsby sickens in body and mind, and feels as if he were going, every moment deeper down, into the infernal gulf.

"Draw off a bit here, Mr. Snagsby," says Bucket, as a

kind of shabby palanquin is borne towards them, surrounded by a noisy crowd. "Here's the fever coming up the street!"

As the unseen wretch goes by, the crowd, leaving that object of attraction, hovers round the three visitors, like a dream of horrible faces, and fades away up alleys and into ruins, and behind walls; and with occasional cries and shrill whistles of warning, thenceforth flits about them till they leave the place.

"Are those the fever-houses, Darby?" Mr. Bucket coolly asks, as he turns his bull's-eye on a line of stinking ruins.

Darby replies that "all them are," and further that in all, for months and months, the people "have been down by dozens," and have been carried out, dead and dying "like sheep with the rot." Bucket observing to Mr. Snagsby as they go on again, that he looks a little poorly, Mr. Snagsby answers that he feels as if he couldn't breathe the dreadful air.

There is inquiry made, at various houses, for a boy named Jo. As few people are known in Tom-all-Alone's by any Christian sign, there is much reference to Mr. Snagsby whether he means Carrots, or the Colonel, or Gallows, or Young Chisel, or Terrier Tip, or Lanky, or the Brick. Mr. Snagsby describes over and over again. There are conflicting opinions respecting the original of his picture. Some think it must be Carrots; some say the Brick. The Colonel is produced, but is not at all near the thing. Whenever Mr. Snagsby and his conductors are stationary, the crowd flows round, and from its squalid depths obsequious advice heaves up to Mr. Bucket. Whenever they move, and the angry bull's-eyes glare, it fades away, and flits about them up the alleys, and in the ruins, and behind the walls, as before.

At last there is a lair found out where Toughy, or the Tough Subject, lays him down at night; and it is thought that the Tough Subject may be Jo. Comparison of notes between Mr. Snagsby and the proprietress of the house—a drunken face tied up in a black bundle, and flaring out of a heap of rags on the floor of a dog hutch which is her private apartment—leads to the establishment of this conclusion. Toughy has gone to the Doctor's to get a bottle of stuff for a sick woman, but will be here anon.

" That's Jo," says Mr. Snagsby.

Jo stands amazed in the disk of light, like a ragged figure in a magic-lantern, trembling to think that he has offended against the law in not having moved on far enough. Mr. Snagsby, however, giving him the consolatory assurance, " It's only a job you will be paid for, Jo," he recovers; and, on being taken outside by Mr. Bucket for a little private confabulation, tells his tale satisfactorily, though out of breath.

" I have squared it with the lad," says Mr. Bucket, returning, " and it's all right. Now, Mr. Snagsby, we're ready for you."

First, Jo has to complete his errand of good-nature by handing over the physic he has been to get, which he delivers with the laconic verbal direction that " it's to be all took d'rectly." Secondly, Mr. Snagsby has to lay upon the table half-a-crown, his usual panacea for an immense variety of afflictions. Thirdly, Mr. Bucket has to take Jo by the arm a little above the elbow and walk him on before him; without which observance, neither the Tough Subject nor any other Subject could be professionally conducted to Lincoln's Inn Fields. These arrangements completed, they give the woman good night, and come out once more into black and foul Tom-all-Alone's.

By the noisome ways through which they descended into that pit, they gradually emerge from it; the crowd flitting, and whistling, and skulking about them, until they come to the verge, where restoration of the bull's eye is made to Darby. Here, the crowd like a concourse of imprisoned demons, turns back, yelling, and is seen no more. Through the clearer and fresher streets, never so clear and fresh to Mr. Snagsby's mind as now, they walk and ride, until they come to Mr. Tulkinghorn's gate.

As they ascend the dim stairs (Mr. Tulkinghorn's chambers being on the first floor), Mr. Bucket mentions that he has the key of the outer door in his pocket, and that there is no need to ring. For a man so expert in most things of that kind, Bucket takes time to open the door, and makes some noise too. It may be that he sounds a note of preparation.

Howbeit, they come at last into the hall, where a lamp is burning, and so into Mr. Tulkinghorn's usual room—the room where he drank his old wine to-night. He is not there, but his two old-fashioned candlesticks are; and the room is tolerably light.

Mr. Bucket, still having his professional hold of Jo, and appearing to Mr. Snagsby to possess an unlimited number of eyes, makes a little way into this room, when Jo starts and stops.

" What's the matter?" said Bucket in a whisper.

" There she is!" cried Jo.

" Who?"

" The lady!"

A female figure, closely veiled, stands in the middle of the room, where the light falls upon it. It is quite still, and silent. The front of the figure is towards them, but it takes no notice of their entrance, and remains like a statue.

" Now, tell me," says Bucket aloud, " how you know that to be the lady."

" I know the wale," replies Jo, staring, " and the bonnet, and the gownd."

" Be quite sure of what you say, Tough," returns Bucket, narrowly observant of him. " Look again."

" I am a-looking as hard as ever I can look," says Jo, with starting eyes, " and that there's the wale, the bonnet, and the gownd."

" What about those rings you told me of?" asks Bucket.

" A-sparkling all over here," says Jo, rubbing the fingers of his left hand on the knuckles of his right, without taking his eyes from the figure.

The figure removes the right-hand glove, and shows the hand.

"Now, what do you say to that?" asks Bucket.

Jo shakes his head. "Not rings a bit like them. Not a hand like that."

"What are you talking of?" says Bucket; evidently pleased though, and well pleased too.

"Hand was a deal whiter, a deal delicater, and a deal smaller," returns Jo.

"Why, you'll tell me I'm my own mother next," says Mr. Bucket. "Do you recollect the lady's voice?"

"I think I does," says Jo.

The figure speaks. "Was it all like this? I will speak as long as you like if you are not sure. Was it this voice, or at all like this voice?"

Jo looks aghast at Mr. Bucket. "Not a bit!"

"Then, what," retorts that worthy, pointing to the figure, "did you say it was the lady for?"

"Cos," says Jo, with a perplexed stare, but without being at all shaken in his certainty, "cos that there's the wale, the bonnet, and the gownd. It is her and it an't her. It an't her hand, nor yet her rings, nor yet her woice. But that there's the wale, the bonnet, and the gownd, and they're wore the same way wot she wore 'em, and it's her height wot she wos, and she giv me a sov'-ring and hooked it."

"Well!" says Mr. Bucket, slightly, "we haven't got much good out of *you*. But, however, here's five shillings for you. Take care how you spend it, and don't get yourself into trouble." Bucket stealthily tells the coins from one hand into the other like counters—which is a way he has, his principal use of them being in these games of skill— and then puts them, in a little pile, into the boy's hand, and takes him out to the door; leaving Mr. Snagsby, not by any means comfortable under these mysterious circumstances, alone with the veiled figure. But on Mr. Tulkinghorn's coming into the room, the veil is raised, and a sufficiently good-looking Frenchwoman is revealed, though her expression is something of the intensest.

"Thank you, Mademoiselle Hortense," says Mr. Tulkinghorn, with his usual equanimity. "I will give you no further trouble about this little wager."

"You will do me the kindness to remember, sir, that I am not at present placed?" says Mademoiselle.

"Certainly, certainly!"

"And to confer upon me the favor of your distinguished recommendation?"

"By all means, Mademoiselle Hortense."

"A word from Mr. Tulkinghorn is so powerful."—"It shall not be wanting, Mademoiselle."—"Receive the assurance of my devoted gratitude, dear sir."—"Good-night." Mademoiselle goes out with an air of native gentility; and Mr. Bucket, to whom it is, on an emergency, as natural to be groom of the ceremonies as it is to be anything else, shows her downstairs, not without gallantry.

"Well, Bucket?" quoth Mr. Tulkinghorn, on his return.

"It's all squared, you see, as I squared it myself, sir. There an't a doubt that it was the other one with this one's dress on. The boy was exact respecting colors and everything. Mr. Snagsby, I promised you as a man that he should be sent away all right. Don't say it wasn't done!"

"You have kept your word, sir," returns the stationer; "and if I can be of no further use, Mr. Tulkinghorn, I think, as my little woman will be getting anxious——"

"Thank you, Snagsby, no further use," says Mr. Tulkinghorn. "I am quite indebted to you for the trouble you have taken already."

"Not at all, sir. I wish you good-night."

"You see, Mr. Snagsby," says Mr. Bucket, accompanying him to the door, and shaking hands with him over and over again, "what I like in you is, that you're a man it's of no use pumping; that's what *you* are. When you know you have done a right thing, you put it away, and it's done with and gone, and there's an end of it. That's what *you* do."

"That is certainly what I endeavor to do, sir," returns Mr. Snagsby.

"No, you don't do yourself justice. It an't what you endeavor to do," says Mr. Bucket, shaking hands with him and blessing him in the tenderest manner, "it's what *you do*. That's what I estimate in a man in your way of business."

Mr. Snagsby makes a suitable response; and goes homeward so confused by the events of the evening, that he is doubtful of his being awake and out—doubtful of the reality of the streets through which he goes—doubtful of the reality of the moon that shines above him. He is presently reassured on these subjects, by the unchallengeable reality of Mrs. Snagsby, sitting up with her head in a perfect bee-hive of curl-papers and nightcap; who has dispatched Guster to the police-station with official intelligence of her husband's being made away with, and who, within the last two hours, has passed through every stage of swooning with the greatest decorum. But, as the little woman feelingly says, many thanks she gets for it!

IX

NATIONAL AND DOMESTIC

ENGLAND has been in a dreadful state for some weeks. Lord Coodle would go out, Sir Thomas Doodle wouldn't come in, and there being nobody in Great Britain (to speak of) except Coodle and Doodle, there has been no Government. It is a mercy that the hostile meeting between those two great men, which at one time seemed inevitable, did not come off; because if both pistols had taken effect, and Coodle and Doodle had killed each other, it is to be presumed that England must have waited to be governed until young Coodle and young Doodle, now in frocks and long stockings, were grown up. The stupendous national calamity, however, was averted by Lord Coodle's making the timely discovery, that if in the heat of debate he had said that he scorned and despised the whole ignoble career of Sir Thomas Doodle, he had merely meant to say that party differences should never induce him to withhold from it the tribute of his warmest admiration; while it as opportunely turned out, on the other hand, that Sir Thomas Doodle had in his own bosom expressly booked Lord Coodle to go down to posterity as the mirror of virtue and honor. Still England has been some weeks in the dismal strait of having no pilot (as was well observed by Sir Leicester Dedlock) to weather the storm; and the marvelous part of the matter is, that England has not appeared to care very much about it, but has gone on eating and drinking and marrying and giving in marriage, as the old world did in the days before the flood. But Coodle knew the danger, and Doodle knew the danger, and all their followers and hangers-on had the clearest possible perception of the danger. At last Sir Thomas Doodle has not only condescended to come in, but has done it handsomely, bringing in with him all his nephews, all his male cousins, and all his brothers-in-law. So there is hope for the old ship yet.

Doodle has found that he must throw himself upon the country—chiefly in the form of sovereigns and beer. In this metamorphosed state he is available in a good many places simultaneously, and can throw himself upon a considerable portion of the country at one time. Britannia being much occupied in pocketing Doodle in the form of sovereigns, and swallowing Doodle in the form of beer. and in swearing herself black in the face that she does neither—plainly to the advancement of her glory and morality—the London season comes to a sudden end, through all the Doodleites and Coodleites dispersing to assist Britannia in those religious exercises.

Hence Mrs. Rouncewell, housekeeper at Chesney Wold, foresees, though no instructions have yet come down, that the family may shortly be expected, together with a pretty large accession of cousins and others who can in any way assist the great Constitutional work. And hence the stately old dame, taking Time by the forelock, leads him up and down the staircases, and along the galleries and passages, and through the rooms, to witness before he grows any older that everything is ready; that floors are rubbed bright, carpets spread, curtains shaken out, beds puffed and patted, still-room and kitchen cleared for action,—all things prepared as beseems the Dedlock dignity.

This present summer evening, as the sun goes down, the preparations are complete. Dreary and solemn the old house looks, with so many appliances of habitation, and with no inhabitants except the pictured forms upon the walls. So did these come and go, a Dedlock in possession might have ruminated passing along; so they did see this gallery hushed and quiet, as I see it now; so think, as I think, of the gap that they would make in this domain when they were gone; so find it, as I find it, difficult to believe that it could be, without them; so pass from my world, as I pass from theirs, now closing the reverberating door; so leave no blank to miss them, and so die.

Through some of the fiery windows, beautiful from without, and set, at this sunset hour, not in dull gray stone but in a glorious house of gold, the light excluded at other windows pours in, rich, lavish, overflowing like the summer plenty in the land. Then do the frozen Dedlocks thaw. Strange movements come upon their features, as the shadows of leaves play there. A dense Justice in a corner is beguiled into a wink. A staring Baronet, with a truncheon, gets a dimple in his chin. Down into the bosom of a stony shepherdess there steals a fleck of light and warmth, that would have done it good, a hundred years ago. One ancestress of Volumnia, in high-heeled shoes, very like her—casting the shadow of that virgin event before her full two centuries—shoots out into a halo and becomes a saint. A maid of honor of the court of Charles the Second, with large round eyes (and other charms to correspond), seems to bathe in glowing water, and it ripples as it glows.

But the fire of the sun is dying. Even now the floor is dusky, and shadow slowly mounts the walls, bringing the

Dedlocks down like age and death. And now, upon my lady's picture over the great chimney-piece, a weird shade falls from some old tree, that turns it pale, and flutters it, and looks as if a great arm held a veil or hood, watching an opportunity to draw it over her. Higher and darker rises the shadow on the wall—now a red gloom on the ceiling—now the fire is out.

All that prospect, which from the terrace looked so near, has moved solemnly away, and changed—not the first nor the last of beautiful things that look so near and will so change—into a distant phantom. Light mists arise, and the dew falls, and all the sweet scents in the garden are heavy in the air. Now, the woods settle into great masses as if they were each one profound tree. And now the moon rises, to separate them, and to glimmer here and there, in horizontal lines behind their stems, and to make the avenue a pavement of light among high cathedral arches fantastically broken.

Now, the moon is high; and the great house, needing habitation more than ever, is like a body without life. Now, it is even awful, stealing through it, to think of the live people who have slept in the solitary bedrooms; to say nothing of the dead. Now is the time for shadow, when every corner is a cavern, and every downward step a pit, when the stained glass is reflected in pale and faded hues upon the floors, when anything and everything can be made of the heavy staircase beams excepting their own proper shapes, when the armor has dull lights upon it not easily to be distinguished from stealthy movement, and when barred helmets are frightfully suggestive of heads inside. But, of all the shadows in Chesney Wold, the shadow in the long drawing-room upon my lady's picture is the first to come, the last to be disturbed. At this hour and by this light it changes into threatening hands raised up, and menacing the handsome face with every breath that stirs.

" She is not well, ma'am," says a groom in Mrs. Rouncewell's audience-chamber.

" My Lady not well! What's the matter?"

"Why, my Lady has been but poorly, ma'am, since she was last here—I don't mean with the family, ma'am, but when she was here as a bird of passage-like. My Lady has not been out much for her, and has kept her room a good deal."

"Chesney Wold, Thomas," rejoins the housekeeper, with proud complacency, "will set my Lady up! There is no finer air, and no healthier soil, in the world!"

Thomas may have his own personal opinions on this subject; probably hints them, in his manner of smoothing his sleek head from the nape of his neck to his temples; but he forbears to express them further, and retires to the servants' hall to regale on cold meat-pie and ale.

This groom is the pilot-fish before the nobler shark. Next evening, down come Sir Leicester and my Lady with their largest retinue, and down come the cousins and others from all the points of the compass. Thenceforth for some weeks, backward and forward rush mysterious men with no names, who fly about all those particular parts of the country on which Doodle is at present throwing himself in an auriferous and malty shower, but who are merely persons of a restless disposition and never do anything anywhere.

On these national occasions, Sir Leicester finds the cousins useful. A better man than the Honorable Bob Stables to meet the Hunt at dinner, there could not possibly be. Better got up gentlemen than the other cousins, to ride over to polling-booths and hustings here and there, and show themselves on the side of England, it would be hard to find.

Then there is Volumnia Dedlock, a young lady (of sixty) who is doubly highly related; being a poor relation, by the mother's side, to another great family.

Volumnia is a little dim, but she is of the true descent; and there are many who appreciate her sprightly conversation, her French conundrums so old as to have become in the cycles of time almost new again, the honor of taking the fair Dedlock into dinner, or even the privilege of her hand in the dance. On these national occasions, dancing may be a patriotic service; and Volumnia is constantly seen hopping about, for the good of an ungrateful and unpensioning country.

My Lady takes no great pains to entertain the numerous guests, and, being still unwell, rarely appears until late in the day. But, at all the dismal dinners, leaden lunches, basilisk balls, and other melancholy pageants, her mere appearance is a relief. As to Sir Leicester, he conceives it utterly impossible that anything can be wanting, in any direction, by anyone who has the good fortune to be received under that roof; and in a state of sublime satisfaction, he moves among the company, a magnificent refrigerator.

Daily the cousins trot through dust, and canter over roadside turf, away to hustings and polling-booths (with leather gloves and hunting-whips for the counties, and kid gloves and riding-canes for the boroughs), and daily bring back reports on which Sir Leicester holds forth after dinner. Daily the restless men who have no occupation in life, present the appearance of being rather busy. Daily, Volumnia has a little cousinly talk with Sir Leicester on the state of the nation, from which Sir Leicester is disposed to conclude that Volumnia is a more reflecting woman than he had thought her.

" How are we getting on? " says Miss Volumnia, clasping her hands. " *Are* we safe? "

The mighty business is nearly over by this time, and Doodle will throw himself on the country in a few days more. Sir Leicester has just appeared in the long drawing-room after dinner; a bright particular star, surrounded by clouds of cousins.

" Volumnia," replies Sir Leicester, who has a list in his hand, " we are doing tolerably."

" Only tolerably! "

Although it is summer weather, Sir Leicester always had his own particular fire in the evening. He takes his usual screened seat near it, and repeats, with much firmness and a little displeasure, as who should say, I am not a common man, and when I say tolerably, it must not be understood as a common expression; " Volumnia, we are doing tolerably."

" At least there is no opposition to *you*," Volumnia asserts with confidence.

" No, Volumnia. This distracted country has lost its senses in many respects, I grieve to say, but——"

" It is not so mad as that. I am glad to hear it!"

Volumnia's finishing the sentence restores her to favor. Sir Leicester, with a gracious inclination of his head, seems to say to himself, " A sensible woman this, on the whole, though occasionally precipitate."

In fact, as to this question of opposition, the fair Dedlock's observation was superfluous: Sir Leicester, on these occasions, always delivering in his own candidateship, as a kind of handsome wholesale order to be promptly executed. Two other little seats that belong to him, he treats as retail orders of less importance; merely sending down the men, and signifying to the tradespeople, " You will have the goodness to make these materials into two members of parliament, and to send them home when done."

" I regret to say, Volumnia, that in many places the people have shown a bad spirit, and that this opposition to the Government has been of a most determined and most implacable description."

" W-r-retches!" says Volumnia.

" Even," proceeds Sir Leicester, glancing at the circumjacent cousins on sofas and ottomans, " even in many—in fact, in most—of those places in which the Government has carried it against a faction——"

(Note, by the way, that the Coodleites are always a faction with the Doodleites, and that the Doodleites occupy exactly the same position towards the Coodleites.)

" —Even in them I am shocked, for the credit of Englishmen, to be constrained to inform you that the Party has not triumphed without being put to an enormous expense. Hundreds," says Sir Leicester, eying the cousins with increasing dignity and swelling indignation, "hundreds of thousands of pounds!"

If Volumnia have a fault, it is the fault of being a trifle too innocent; seeing that the innocence which would go extremely well with a sash and tucker, is a little out of keeping with rouge and pearl necklace. Howbeit, impelled by innocence, she asks:

"What for?"

"Volumnia," remonstrates Sir Leicester, with his utmost severity. "Volumnia!"

"No, no, I don't mean what for," cries Volumnia, with her favorite little scream. "How stupid I am! I mean what a pity!"

"I am glad," returns Sir Leicester, "that you do mean what a pity."

Volumnia hastens to express her opinion that the shocking people ought to be tried as traitors, and made to support the Party.

"I am glad, Volumnia," repeats Sir Leicester, unmindful of these mollifying sentiments, "that you do mean what a pity. It is disgraceful to the electors. But as you, though inadvertently, and without intending so unreasonable a question, asked me 'what for?' let me reply to you. For necessary expenses. And I trust to your good sense, Volumnia, not to pursue the subject, here or elsewhere."

Sir Leicester feels it incumbent on him to observe a crushing aspect towards Volumnia, because it is whispered abroad that these necessary expenses will, in some two hundred election petitions, be unpleasantly connected with the word bribery; and because some graceless jokers have consequently suggested the omission from the Church service of the ordinary supplication in behalf of the High Court of Parliament, and have recommended instead that the prayers of the congregation be requested for six hundred and fifty-eight gentlemen in a very unhealthy state.

"I suppose," observes Volumnia, having taken a little time to recover her spirits after her late castigation, "I suppose Mr. Tulkinghorn has been worked to death."

" I don't know," says Sir Leicester, opening his eyes, " why Mr. Tulkinghorn should be worked to death. I don't know what Mr. Tulkinghorn's engagements may be. He is not a candidate."

Volumnia had thought he might have been employed. Sir Leicester could desire to know by whom, and what for? Volumnia, abashed again, suggests, by Somebody—to advise and make arrangements. Sir Leicester is not aware that any client of Mr. Tulkinghorn has been in need of his assistance.

Lady Dedlock, seated at an open window with her arm upon its cushioned ledge and looking out at the evening shadows falling on the park, has seemed to attend since the lawyer's name was mentioned.

A languid cousin with a mustache, in a state of extreme debility, now observes from his couch, that—man told him ya'as'dy that Tulkinghorn had gone down t' that iron place t' give legal 'pinion 'bout something; and that, contest being over t' day, 'twould be highly jawlly thing if Tulkinghorn should 'pear with news that Coodle man was floored.

Mercury in attendance with coffee informs Sir Leicester, hereupon, that Mr. Tulkinghorn has arrived, and has taken dinner. My Lady turns her head inward for the moment, then looks out again as before.

Volumnia is charmed to hear that her Delight is come. He is so original, such a stolid creature, such an immense being for knowing all sorts of things and never telling them! Volumnia is persuaded that he must be a Freemason. Is sure he is at the head of a lodge, wears short aprons, and is made a perfect Idol of, with candlesticks and trowels. These lively remarks the fair Dedlock delivers in her youthful manner, while making a purse.

" He has not been here once," she adds, " since I came. I really had some thoughts of breaking my heart for the Inconstant creature. I had almost made up my mind that he was dead."

It may be the gathering gloom of evening, or it may be

the darker gloom within herself, but a shade is on my Lady's face, as if she thought, " I would he were! "

" Mr. Tulkinghorn," says Sir Leicester, " is always welcome here, and always discreet wheresoever he is. A very valuable person, and deservedly respected."

The debilitated cousin supposes he is " 'normously rich fler."

" He has a stake in the country," says Sir Leicester, " I have no doubt. He is, of course, handsomely paid, and he associates almost on a footing of equality with the highest society."

Everybody starts. For a gun is fired close by.

" Good gracious, what's that? " cries Volumnia with her little withered scream.

" A rat," says my Lady. " And they have shot him."

Enter Mr. Tulkinghorn, followed by Mercuries with lamps and candles.

" No, no," says Sir Leicester, " I think not. My lady, do you object to the twilight? "

On the contrary, my Lady prefers it.

" Volumnia? "

O! nothing is so delicious to Volumnia, as to sit and talk in the dark.

" Then take them away," says Sir Leicester. " Tulkinghorn, I beg your pardon. How do you do? "

Mr. Tulkinghorn with his usual leisurely ease advances, renders his passing homage to my Lady, takes Sir Leicester's hand, and subsides into the chair proper to him when he has anything to communicate, on the opposite side of the Baronet's little newspaper-table. Sir Leicester is apprehensive that my Lady, not being very well, will take cold at that open window. My Lady is obliged to him, but would rather sit there, for the air. Sir Leicester rises, adjusts her scarf about her, and returns to his seat. Mr. Tulkinghorn in the meanwhile takes a pinch of snuff.

" Now," says Sir Leicester. " How has that contest gone? "

" Oh, hollow from the beginning. Not a chance. They

have brought in both their people. You are beaten out of all reason. Three to one."

It is a part of Mr. Tulkinghorn's policy and mastery to have *no* political opinions; indeed, *no* opinions. Therefore he says " you " are beaten, and not " we."

Sir Leicester is majestically wroth. Volumnia never heard of such a thing. The debilitated cousin holds that it's— sort of thing that's pure tapu slongs votes—giv'n—Mob.

" It's the place, you know," Mr. Tulkinghorn goes on to say in the last increasing darkness, when there is silence again, " where they wanted to put up Mrs. Rouncewell's son."

" A proposal which, as you correctly informed me at the time, he had the becoming taste and perception," observes Sir Leicester, " to decline. I cannot say that I by any means approve of the sentiments expressed by Mr. Rouncewell, some little while ago, when he requested Lady Dedlock to part with her young companion, simply because his son was attached to the girl. Yet there was a sense of propriety in his decision."

" Ha! " says Mr. Tulkinghorn. " It did not prevent him from being very active in this election, though."

Sir Leicester is distinctly heard to gasp before speaking. " Did I understand you? Did you say that Mr. Rouncewell had been very active in this election? "

" Uncommonly active."

" Against—— "

" O dear yes, against you. He is a very good speaker. Plain and emphatic. He made a damaging effect, and has great influence. In the business-part of the proceedings he carried all before him."

It is evident to the whole company, though nobody can see him, that Sir Leicester is staring majestically.

" And he was much assisted," says Mr. Tulkinghorn, as a wind-up, " by his son."

" By his son, sir? " repeats Sir Leicester, with awful politeness.

" By his son."

" The son who wished to marry the young woman in my Lady's service?'

" That son. He has but one."

" Then upon my honor," says Sir Leicester, after a terrific pause, during which he has been heard to snort and felt to stare; " then upon my honor, upon my life, upon my reputation and principles, the floodgates of society are burst open, and the waters have—a—obliterated the landmarks of the framework of the cohesion by which things are held together ! "

General burst of cousinly indignation. Volumnia thinks it is really high time, you know, for somebody in power to step in and do something strong. Debilitated cousin thinks —Country's going—DAYVLE—steeple-chase pace.

" I beg," says Sir Leicester, in a breathless condition, " that we may not comment further on this circumstance. Comment is superfluous. My Lady, let me suggest in reference to that young woman——"

" I have no intention," observes my Lady from her window, in a low but decided tone, " of parting with her."

" That was not my meaning," returns Sir Leicester.   " I am glad to hear you say so. I would suggest that as you think her worthy of your patronage, you should exert your influence to keep her from these dangerous hands. You might show her what violence would be done, in such association, to her duties and principles; and you might preserve her for a better fate. You might point out to her that she probably would, in good time, find a husband at Chesney Wold by whom she would not be——" Sir Leicester adds, after a moment's consideration, " dragged from the altars of her forefathers."

These remarks he offers with his unvarying politeness and deference when he addresses himself to his wife. She merely moves her head in reply. The moon is rising; and where she sits there is a little stream of cold pale light, in which her head is seen.

" It is worthy of remark," says Mr. Tulkinghorn, " however, that these people are, in their way, very proud."

"Proud?" Sir Leicester doubts his hearing.

"I should not be surprised, if they all voluntarily abandoned the girl—yes, lover and all—instead of her abandoning them, supposing she remained at Chesney Wold under such circumstances."

"Well!" says Sir Leicester, tremulously, "Well! You should know, Mr. Tulkinghorn. You have been among them."

"Really, Sir Leicester," returns the lawyer, "I state the fact. Why, I could tell you a story—with Lady Dedlock's permission."

Her head concedes it, and Volumnia is enchanted. A story! O he is going to tell something at last! A ghost in it, Volumnia hopes?

"No. Real flesh and blood." Mr. Tulkinghorn stops for an instant, and repeats, with some little emphasis grafted upon his usual monotony, "Real flesh and blood, Miss Dedlock. Sir Leicester, these particulars have only lately become known to me. They are very brief. They exemplify what I have said. I suppress names for the present. Lady Dedlock will not think me ill-bred, I hope?"

By the light of the fire, which is low, he can be seen looking towards the moonlight. By the light of the moon Lady Dedlock can be seen, perfectly still.

"A townsman of this Mrs. Rouncewell, a man in exactly parallel circumstances as I am told, had the good fortune to have a daughter who attracted the notice of a great lady. I speak of really a great lady; not merely great to him, but married to a gentleman of your condition, Sir Leicester."

Sir Leicester condescendingly says, "Yes, Mr. Tulkinghorn;" implying that then she must have appeared of very considerable moral dimensions indeed, in the eyes of an ironmaster.

"The lady was wealthy and beautiful, and had a liking for the girl, and treated her with great kindness, and kept her always near her. Now this lady preserved a secret under all her greatness, which she had preserved for many years. In fact, she had in early life been engaged to marry a young rake—he was a captain in the army—nothing connected with whom came to any good. She never did marry him, but she gave birth to a child of which he was the father."

By the light of the fire he can be seen looking towards the moonlight. By the moonlight, Lady Dedlock can be seen in profile, perfectly still.

" The captain in the army being dead, she believed herself safe; but a train of circumstances with which I need not trouble you, led to discovery. As I received the story, they began in an imprudence on her own part one day, when she was taken by surprise; which shows how difficult it is for the firmest of us (she was very firm) to be always guarded. There was great domestic trouble and amazement, you may suppose; I leave you to imagine, Sir Leicester, the husband's grief. But that is not the present point. When Mr. Rouncewell's townsman heard of the disclosure, he no more allowed the girl to be patronized and honored, than he would have suffered her to be trodden underfoot before his eyes. Such was his pride, that he indignantly took her away, as if from reproach and disgrace. He had no sense of the honor done him and his daughter by the lady's condescension; not the least. He resented the girl's position, as if the lady had been the commonest of commoners. That is the story. I hope Lady Dedlock will excuse its painful nature."

There are various opinions on the merits, more or less conflicting with Volumnia's. That fair young creature cannot believe there ever was any such lady, and rejects the whole history on the threshold. The majority incline to the debilitated cousin's sentiment, which is in few words — "no business — Rouncewell's fernal townsman." Sir Leicester generally refers back in his mind to Wat Tyler, and arranges a sequence of events on a plan of his own.

There is not much conversation in all, for late hours have been kept at Chesney Wold since the necessary expenses elsewhere began, and this is the first night in many on which the family have been alone. It is past ten, when Sir

Leicester begs Mr. Tulkinghorn to ring for candles. Then the stream of moonlight has swelled into a lake, and then Lady Dedlock for the first time moves, and rises, and comes forward to a table for a glass of water. Winking cousins, bat-like in the candle glare, crowd round to give it; Volumnia (always ready for something better if procurable) takes another, a very mild sip of which contents her; Lady Dedlock, graceful, self-possessed, looked after by admiring eyes, passes away slowly down the long perspective by the side of that Nymph, not at all improving her as a question of contrast.

X

IN MR. TULKINGHORN'S ROOM

MR. TULKINGHORN arrives in his turret-room, a little breathed by the journey up, though leisurely performed. There is an expression on his face as if he had discharged his mind of some grave matter, and were, in his close way, satisfied. To say of a man so severely and strictly self-repressed that he is triumphant, would be to do him as great an injustice as to suppose him troubled with love or sentiment, or any romantic weakness. He is sedately satisfied. Perhaps there is a rather increased sense of power upon him, as he loosely grasps one of his veinous wrists with his other hand, and holding it behind his back walks noiselessly up and down.

There is a capacious writing-table in the room, on which is a pretty large accumulation of papers. The green lamp is lighted, his reading-glasses lie upon the desk, the easy-chair is wheeled up to it, and it would seem as though he had intended to bestow an hour or so upon these claims on his attention before going to bed. But he happens not to be in a business mind. After a glance at the documents awaiting his notice—with his head bent low over the table, the old man's sight for print or writing being defective at night—he opens the French window and steps out upon the leads. There he again walks slowly up and down, in the same attitude; subsiding, if a man so cool may have any need to subside, from the story he has related downstairs.

The time was once, when men as knowing as Mr. Tulkinghorn would walk on turret-tops in the star-light, and look up into the sky to read their fortunes there. Hosts of stars are visible to-night, though their brilliancy is eclipsed by the splendor of the moon. If he be seeking his own star, as he methodically turns and turns upon the leads, it should be but a pale one to be so rustily represented below. If he be tracing out his destiny, that may be written in other characters nearer to his hand.

As he paces the leads, with his eyes most probably as high above his thoughts as they are high above the earth, he is suddenly stopped in passing the window by two eyes that meet his own. The ceiling of his room is rather low: the upper part of the door, which is opposite the window, is of glass. There is an inner baize door, too, but the night being warm he did not close it when he came upstairs. These eyes that meet his own, are looking in through the glass from the corridor outside. He knows them well. The blood has not flushed into his face so suddenly and readily for many a long year, as when he recognizes Lady Dedlock.

He steps into the room, and she comes in too, closing both the doors behind her. There is a wild disturbance—is it fear or anger?—in her eyes. In her carriage and all else, she looks as she looked downstairs two hours ago.

Is it fear, or is it anger, now? He cannot be sure. Both might be as pale, both as intent.

"Lady Dedlock?"

She does not speak at first, nor even when she has slowly dropped into the easy-chair by the table. They look at each other, like two pictures.

"Why have you told my story to so many persons?"

"Lady Dedlock, it was necessary for me to inform you that I knew it."

"How long have you known it?"

" I have suspected it a long while—fully known it a little while."

" Months? "

" Days."

He stands before her, with one hand on a chair-back and the other in his old-fashioned waistcoat and shirt-frill, exactly as he has stood before her at any time since her marriage. The same formal politeness, the same composed deference that might as well be defiance; the whole man the same dark, cold object, at the same distance, which nothing has ever diminished.

" Is this true concerning the poor girl? "

He slightly inclines and advances his head, as not quite understanding the question.

" You know what you related. Is it true? Do her friends know my story also? Is it the town-talk yet? Is it chalked upon the walls and cried in the streets? "

So! Anger, and fear, and shame. All three contending. What power this woman has to keep these raging passions down! Mr. Tulkinghorn's thoughts take such form as he looks at her, with his ragged gray eyebrows a hair's-breadth more contracted than usual, under her gaze.

" No, Lady Dedlock. That was a hypothetical case, arising out of Sir Leicester's unconsciously carrying the matter with so high a hand. But it would be a real case if they knew—what we know."

" Then they do not know it yet? "

" No."

" Can I save the poor girl from injury before they know it? "

" Really, Lady Dedlock," Mr. Tulkinghorn replies, " I cannot give a satisfactory opinion on that point."

And he thinks, with the interest of attentive curiosity, as he watches the struggle in her breast, " The power and force of this woman are astonishing! "

" Sir," she says, for the moment obliged to set her lips with all the energy she has, that she may speak distinctly, " I will make it plainer. I do not dispute your hypothetical case. I anticipated it, and felt its truth as strongly as you can do, when I saw Mr. Rouncewell here. I knew very well that if he could have had the power of seeing me as I was, he would consider the poor girl tarnished by having for a moment been, although most innocently, the subject of my great and distinguished patronage. But, I have an interest in her; or I should rather say—no longer belonging to this place—I had; and if you can find so much consideration for the woman under your foot as to remember that, she will be very sensible of your mercy."

Mr. Tulkinghorn, profoundly attentive, throws this off with a shrug of self-depreciation, and contracts his eyebrows a little more.

"You have prepared me for my exposure, and I thank you for that too. Is there anything that you require of me? Is there any claim that I can release, or any charge or trouble that I can spare my husband in obtaining *his* release, by certifying to the exactness of your discovery? I will write anything, here and now, that you will dictate. I am ready to do it."

And she would do it! thinks the lawyer, watchful of the firm hand with which she takes the pen!

"I will not trouble you, Lady Dedlock. Pray spare yourself."

"I have long expected this, as you know. I neither wish to spare myself, nor to be spared. You can do nothing worse to me than you have done. Do what remains, now."

"Lady Dedlock, there is nothing to be done. I will take leave to say a few words, when you have finished."

Their need for watching one another should be over now, but they do it all this time, and the stars watch them both through the opened window. Away in the moonlight lie the woodland fields at rest, and the wide house is as quiet as the narrow one. The narrow one! Where are the digger and the spade, this peaceful night, destined to add the last great secret to the many secrets of the Tulkinghorn existence? Is the man born yet, is the spade wrought yet?

Curious questions to consider, more curious perhaps not to consider, under the watching stars upon a summer night.

"Of repentance or remorse, or any feeling of mine," Lady Dedlock presently proceeds, "I say not a word. If I were not dumb, you would be deaf. Let that go by. It is not for your ears."

He makes a feint of offering a protest, but she sweeps it away with her disdainful hand.

"Of other and very different things I come to speak to you. My jewels are all in their proper places of keeping. They will be found there. So, my dresses. So, all the valuables I have. Some ready money I had with me, please to say, but no large amount. I did not wear my own dress, in order that I might avoid observation. I went, to be henceforward lost. Make this known. I leave no other charge with you."

"Excuse me, Lady Dedlock," says Mr. Tulkinghorn, quite unmoved. "I am not sure that I understand you. You went——?"

"To be lost to all here. I leave Chesney Wold to-night. I go this hour."

Mr. Tulkinghorn shakes his head. She rises; but he, without moving hand from chair-back or from old-fashioned waistcoat and shirt-frill, shakes his head.

"What? Not go as I have said?"

"No, Lady Dedlock," he very calmly replies.

"Do you know the relief that my disappearance will be? Have you forgotten the stain and blot upon this place, and where it is, and who it is?"

"No, Lady Dedlock, not by any means."

Without deigning to rejoin, she moves to the inner door and has it in her hand, when he says to her, without himself stirring hand or foot, or raising his voice:

"Lady Dedlock, have the goodness to stop and hear me, or before you reach the staircase I shall ring the alarm-bell and rouse the house. And then I must speak out, before every guest and servant, every man and woman, in it."

He has conquered her. She falters, trembles, and puts her hand confusedly to her head. Slight tokens these in anyone else; but when so practiced an eye as Mr. Tulkinghorn's sees indecision for a moment in such a subject, he thoroughly knows its value.

He promptly says again, " Have the goodness to hear me, Lady Dedlock," and motions to the chair from which she has risen. She hesitates, but he motions again, and she sits down.

"The relations between us are of an unfortunate description, Lady Dedlock; but, as they are not of my making, I will not apologize for them. The position I hold in reference to Sir Leicester is so well known to you, that I can hardly imagine but that I must long have appeared in your eyes the natural person to make this discovery."

" Sir," she returns without looking up from the ground, on which her eyes are now fixed, " I had better have gone. It would have been far better not to have detained me. I have no more to say."

"Excuse me, Lady Dedlock, if I add, a little more to hear."

" I wish to hear it at the window, then; I can't breathe where I am."

His jealous glance as she walks that way, betrays an instant's misgiving that she may have it in her thoughts to leap over, and dashing against ledge and cornice, strike her life out upon the terrace below. But, a moment's observation of her figure as she stands in the window without any support, looking out at the stars—not up—gloomily out at those stars which are low in the heavens—reassures him. By facing round as she has moved, he stands a little behind her.

" Lady Dedlock, I have not yet been able to come to a decision satisfactory to myself, on the course before me. I am not clear what to do, or how to act next. I must request you, in the meantime, to keep your secret as you have kept it so long, and not to wonder that I keep it too."

He pauses, but she makes no reply.

"Pardon me, Lady Dedlock. This is an important subject. You are honoring me with your attention?"

"I am."

"Thank you. I might have known it, from what I have seen of your strength of character. I ought not to have asked the question, but I have the habit of making sure of my ground, step by step, as I go on. The sole consideration in this unhappy case is Sir Leicester."

"Then why," she asks in a low voice, and without removing her gloomy look from those distant stars, "do you detain me in his house?"

"Because he *is* the consideration. Lady Dedlock, I have no occasion to tell you that Sir Leicester is a very proud man; that his reliance upon you is implicit; that the fall of that moon out of the sky, would not amaze him more than your fall from your high position as his wife."

She breathes quickly and heavily, but she stands as unflinchingly as ever he has seen her in the midst of her grandest company.

"I declare to you, Lady Dedlock, that with anything short of this case that I have, I would as soon have hoped to root up, by means of my own strength and my own hands, the oldest tree on this estate, as to shake your hold upon Sir Leicester, and Sir Leicester's trust and confidence in you. And even now, with this case, I hesitate. Not that he could doubt (that, even with him, is impossible), but that nothing can prepare him for the blow."

"Not my flight?" she returned. "Think of it again."

"Your flight, Lady Dedlock, would spread the whole truth, and a hundred times the whole truth, far and wide. It would be impossible to save the family credit for a day. It is not to be thought of."

There is a quiet decision in his reply, which admits of no remonstrance.

"When I speak of Sir Leicester being the sole consideration, he and the family credit are one. Sir Leicester and the baronetcy, Sir Leicester and Chesney Wold, Sir Leicester and his ancestors and his patrimony;" Mr. Tulkinghorn very dry here; " are, I need not say to you, Lady Dedlock, inseparable."

" Good."

" Therefore," says Mr. Tulkinghorn, pursuing his case in his jog-trot style, " I have much to consider. This is to be hushed up, if it can be. How can it be, if Sir Leicester is driven out of his wits, or laid upon a death-bed? If I inflicted this shock upon him to-morrow morning, how could the immediate change in him be accounted for? What could have caused it? What could have divided you? Lady Dedlock, the wall-chalking and the street-crying would come on directly; and you are to remember that it would not affect you merely (whom I cannot at all consider in this business) but your husband, Lady Dedlock, your husband."

He gets plainer as he gets on, but not an atom more emphatic or animated.

" There is another point of view," he continues, " in which the case presents itself. Sir Leicester is devoted to you almost to infatuation. He might not be able to overcome that infatuation, even knowing what we know. I am putting an extreme case, but it might be so. If so, it were better that he knew nothing. Better for common sense, better for him, better for me. I must take all this into account, and it combines to render a decision very difficult."

She stands looking out at the same stars without a word. They are beginning to pale, and she looks as if their coldness froze her.

" My experience teaches me," says Mr. Tulkinghorn, who has by this time got his hands in his pockets, and is going on in his business consideration of the matter, like a machine, " my experience teaches me, Lady Dedlock, that most of the people I know would do far better to leave marriage alone. It is at the bottom of three-fourths of their troubles. So I thought when Sir Leicester married, and so I always have thought since. No more about that. I must now be guided by circumstances. In the meanwhile I must beg you to keep your own counsel, and I will keep mine."

" I am to drag my present life on, holding its pains at your pleasure, day by day?" she asks, still looking at the distant sky.

" Yes, I am afraid so, Lady Dedlock."

" It is necessary, you think, that I should be so tied to the stake?"

" I am sure that what I recommend is necessary."

" I am to remain on this gaudy platform, on which my miserable deception has been so long acted, and it is to fall beneath me when you give the signal?" she said slowly.

" Not without notice, Lady Dedlock. I shall take no step without forewarning you."

She asks all her questions as if she were repeating them from memory, or calling them over in her sleep.

" We are to meet as usual?"

" Precisely as usual, if you please?"

" And I am to hide my guilt, as I have done so many years?"

" As you have done so many years. I should not have made that reference myself, Lady Dedlock, but I may now remind you that your secret can be no heavier to you than it was, and is no worse and no better than it was. *I* know it certainly, but I believe we have never wholly trusted each other."

She stands absorbed in the same frozen way for some little time, before asking:

" Is there anything more to be said to-night?"

" Why," Mr. Tulkinghorn returns methodically as he softly rubs his hands, " I should like to be assured of your acquiescence in my arrangements, Lady Dedlock."

" You may be assured of it."

" Good. And I would wish in conclusion to remind you, as a business precaution, in case it should be necessary to recall the fact in any communication with Sir Leicester, that throughout our interview I have expressly stated my sole consideration to be Sir Leicester's feelings and honor, and the family reputation. I should have been happy to have made Lady Dedlock a prominent consideration, too, if the case had admitted of it; but unfortunately it does not."

" I can attest your fidelity, sir."

Both before and after saying it she remains absorbed, but at length moves, and turns, unshaken in her natural and acquired presence, towards the door. Mr. Tulkinghorn opens both the doors exactly as he would have done yesterday, or as he would have done ten years ago, and makes his old-fashioned bow as she passes out. It is not an ordinary look that he receives from the handsome face as it goes into the darkness, and it is not an ordinary movement, though a very slight one, that acknowledges his courtesy. But, as he reflects when he is left alone, the woman has been putting no common constraint upon herself.

He would know it all the better, if he saw the woman pacing her own rooms with her hair wildly thrown from her flung back face, her hands clasped behind her head, her figure twisted as if by pain. He would think so all the more, if he saw the woman thus hurrying up and down for hours, without fatigue, without intermission, followed by the faithful step upon the Ghost's Walk. But he shuts out the now chilled air, draws the window-curtain, goes to bed, and falls asleep. And truly when the stars go out and the wan day peeps into the turret-chamber, finding him at his oldest, he looks as if the digger and the spade were both commissioned, and would soon be digging.

The same wan day peeps in at Sir Leicester pardoning the repentant country in a majestically condescending dream; and at the cousins entering on various public employments, principally receipt of salary; and at the chaste Volumnia, bestowing a dower of fifty thousand pounds upon a hideous old General, with a mouth of false teeth like a pianoforte too full of keys, long the admiration of Bath and the terror of every other community. Also into rooms high in the roof, and into offices in court-yards and over stables, where humbler ambition dreams of bliss, in keepers' lodges, and in holy matrimony with Will or Sally. Up comes the bright sun, drawing everything up with it—the

Wills and Sallys, the latent vapor in the earth, the drooping leaves and flowers, the birds and beasts and creeping things, the gardeners to sweep the dewy turf and unfold emerald velvet where the roller passes, the smoke of the great kitchen fire wreathing itself straight and high into the lightsome air. Lastly, up comes the flag over Mr. Tulkinghorn's unconscious head, cheerfully proclaiming that Sir Leicester and Lady Dedlock are in their happy home, and that there is hospitality at the place in Lincolnshire.

XI

IN MR. TULKINGHORN'S CHAMBERS

FROM the verdant undulations and the spreading oaks of the Dedlock property, Mr. Tulkinghorn transfers himself to the stale heat and dust of London. His manner of coming and going between the two places, is one of his impenetrabilities. He walks into Chesney Wold as if it were next door to his chambers, and returns to his chambers as if he had never been out of Lincoln's Inn Fields. He neither changes his dress before the journey, nor talks of it afterwards. He melted out of his turret-room this morning, just as now, in the late twilight, he melts into his own square.

Like a dingy London bird among the birds at roost in these pleasant fields, where the sheep are all made into parchment, the goats into wigs, and the pasture into chaff, the lawyer, smoke-dried and faded, dwelling among mankind but not consorting with them, aged without experience of genial youth, and so long used to make his cramped nest in holes and corners of human nature that he has forgotten its broader and better range, comes sauntering home. In the oven made by the hot pavements and hot buildings, he has baked himself dryer than usual; and he has, in his thirsty mind, his mellowed port-wine half a century old.

The lamplighter is skipping up and down his ladder on Mr. Tulkinghorn's side of the Fields, when that high-priest of noble mysteries arrives at his own dull court-yard. He ascends the door-steps, and is gliding into the dusky hall, when he encounters, on the top step, a bowing and propitiatory little man.

" Is that Snagsby?"

" Yes sir. I hope you are well sir. I was just giving you up, sir, and going home."

" Aye? What is it? What do you want with me?"

" Well, sir," says Mr. Snagsby, holding his hat at the side of his head, in his deference towards his best customer, " I was wishful to say a word to you, sir."

" Can you say it here?"

" Perfectly, sir."

" Say it then." The lawyer turns, leans his arms on the iron railing at the top of the steps, and looks at the lamp-lighter lighting the court-yard.

" It is relating," says Mr. Snagsby, in a mysterious low voice: " it is relating—not to put too fine a point upon it—to the foreigner, sir?"

Mr. Tulkinghorn eyes him with some surprise. " What foreigner?"

" The foreign female, sir. French, if I don't mistake. I am not acquainted with that language myself, but I should judge from her manners and appearance that she was French; anyways, certainly foreign. Her that was up-stairs, sir, when Mr. Bucket and me had the honor of waiting upon you with the sweeping-boy that night."

" Oh! yes, yes. Mademoiselle Hortense."

" Indeed, sir?" Mr. Snagsby coughs his cough of submission behind his hat. " I am not acquainted myself with the names of foreigners in general, but I have no doubt it *would* be that." Mr. Snagsby appears to have set out in this reply with some desperate design of repeating the name; but on reflection coughs again to excuse himself.

" And what can you have to say, Snagsby," demands Mr. Tulkinghorn, " about her?"

" Well, sir," returns the stationer, shading his communication with his hat, " it falls a little hard upon me. My domestic happiness is very great—at least, it's as great as can be expected, I'm sure—but my little woman is rather given to jealousy. Not to put too fine a point upon it, she is very much given to jealousy. And you see, a foreign female of that genteel appearance coming into the shop, and hovering—I should be the last to make use of a strong expression, if I could avoid it, but hovering sir—in the court—you know it is—now ain't it? I only put it to yourself, sir."

Mr. Snagsby having said this in a very plaintive manner, throws in a cough of general application to fill up all the blanks.

"Why, what do you mean?" asks Mr. Tulkinghorn.

"Just so, sir," returns Mr. Snagsby; "I was sure you would feel it yourself, and would excuse the reasonableness of *my* feelings when coupled with the known exciteableness of my little woman. You see, the foreign female—which you mentioned her name just now, with quite a native sound, I am sure—caught up the word Snagsby that night, being uncommon quick, and made inquiry, and got the direction and come at dinner-time. Now Guster, our young woman, is timid and has fits, and she, taking fright at the foreigner's looks—which are fierce—and at a grinding manner that she has of speaking—which is calculated to alarm a weak mind—gave way to it, instead of bearing up against it, and tumbled down the kitchen stairs out of one into another, such fits as I do sometimes think are never gone into, or come out of, in any house but ours. Consequently there was by good fortune ample occupation for my little woman, and only me to answer the shop. When she *did* say that Mr. Tulkinghorn, being always denied to her by his employer (which I had no doubt at the time was a foreign mode of viewing a clerk), she would do herself the pleasure of continually calling at my place until she was let in here. Since then she has been, as I began by saying, hovering—hovering, sir," Mr. Snagsby repeats the words with pathetic emphasis, "in the court. The effects of which movement it is impossible to calculate.

I shouldn't wonder if it might have already given rise to the painfullest mistakes even in the neighbors' minds, not mentioning (if such a thing was possible) my little woman. Whereas, goodness knows," says Mr. Snagsby, shaking his head, " I never had an idea of a foreign female, except as being formerly connected with a bunch of brooms and a baby, or at the present time with a tambourine and ear-rings. I never had, I do assure you, sir!"

Mr. Tulkinghorn had listened gravely to this complaint, and inquires, when the stationer has finished, " And that's all, is it, Snagsby?"

" Why, yes, sir, that's all," says Mr. Snagsby, ending with a cough that plainly adds, " and it's enough too—for me."

" I don't know what Mademoiselle Hortense may want or mean, unless she is mad," says the lawyer.

" Even if she was, you know, sir," Mr. Snagsby pleads, " it wouldn't be a consolation to have some weapon or another in the form of a foreign dagger, planted in the family."

" No," says the other. " Well, well! This shall be stopped. I am sorry you have been inconvenienced. If she comes again, send her here."

Mr. Snagsby, with much bowing and short apologetic coughing, takes his leave, lightened in heart. Mr. Tulkinghorn goes upstairs, saying to himself, " These women were created to give trouble, the whole earth over. The mistress not being enough to deal with, here's the maid now! But I will be short with *this* jade at least!"

So saying he unlocks his door, gropes his way into his murky rooms, lights his candles, and looks about him. It is too dark to see much of the allegory overhead there; but that importunate Roman, who is for ever toppling out of the clouds and pointing, is at his old work pretty distinctly. Not honoring him with much attention, Mr. Tulkinghorn takes a small key from his pocket, unlocks a drawer in which there is another key, which unlocks a chest in which there is another, and so comes to the cellar-key, with which he prepares to descend to the regions of old wine. He is going towards the door with a candle in his hand, when a knock comes.

"Who's this?—Aye, aye, mistress, it's you, is it? You appear at a good time. I have just been hearing of you. Now! What do you want?"

He stands the candle on the chimney-piece in the clerk's hall, and taps his dry cheek with the key, as he addresses these words of welcome to Mademoiselle Hortense. That feline personage, with her lips tightly shut, and her eyes looking out at him sideways, softly closes the door before replying.

"I have had great deal of trouble to find you, sir."

"*Have* you!"

"I have been here very often, sir. It has always been said to me, he is not at home, he is engage, he is this and that, he is not for you."

"Quite right, and quite true."

"Not true. Lies!"

At times, there is a suddenness in the manner of Mademoiselle Hortense so like a bodily spring upon the subject of it, that such subject involuntarily starts and falls back. It is Mr. Tulkinghorn's case at present, though Mademoiselle Hortense, with her eyes almost shut up (but still looking out sideways), is only smiling contemptuously and shaking her head.

"Now, mistress," says the lawyer, tapping the key hastily upon the chimney-piece. "If you have anything to say, say it, say it."

"Sir, you have not use me well. You have been mean and shabby."

"Mean and shabby, eh?" returns the lawyer, rubbing his nose with the key.

"Yes. What is it that I tell you? You know you have. You have attrapped me—catched me—to give you information; you have asked me to show you the dress of mine my Lady must have wore that night, you have prayed me to come in here to meet that boy—Say! Is it not?" Mademoiselle Hortense makes another spring.

" You are a vixen, a vixen!" Mr. Tulkinghorn seems to meditate, as he looks distrustfully at her; then he replies, " Well, wench, well. I paid you."

" You paid me!" she repeats, with fierce disdain. " Two sovereign! I have not change them, I ref-use them, I des-pise them, I throw them from me!" Which she liter-ally does, taking them out of her bosom as she speaks, and flinging them with such violence on the floor, that they jerk up again into the light before they roll away into corners, and slowly settle down there after spinning vehemently.

" Now!" says Mademoiselle Hortense, darkening her large eyes again. " You have paid me? Eh my God, O yes!"

Mr. Tulkinghorn rubs his head with the key, while she entertains herself with a sarcastic laugh.

" You must be rich, my fair friend," he composedly ob-serves, " to throw money about in that way!"

" I *am* rich," she returns, " I am very rich in hate. I hate my Lady, of all my heart. You know that."

" Know it? How should I know it?"

" Because you have known it perfectly, before you prayed me to give you that information. Because you have known perfectly that I was en-r-r-r-aged!" It appears impos-sible for Mademoiselle to roll the letter r sufficiently in this word, notwithstanding that she assists her energetic delivery, by clenching both her hands, and setting all her teeth.

" Oh! I knew that, did I?" says Mr. Tulkinghorn, examining the wards of the key.

" Yes, without doubt. I am not blind. You have made sure of me because you knew that. You had reason! I det-est her." Mademoiselle folds her arms, and throws this last remark at him over one of her shoulders.

" Having said this, have you anything else to say, Mademoiselle?"

" I am not yet placed. Place me well. Find me a good condition! If you cannot, or do not choose to do that, em-ploy me to pursue her, to chase her, to disgrace and to dishonor her. I will help you well, and with a good will. It is what *you* do. Do I know that?"

"You appear to know a good deal," Mr. Tulkinghorn retorts.

"Do I not? Is it that I am so weak as to believe, like a child, that I come here in that dress to rec-eive that boy, only to decide a little bet, a wager?—Eh my God, O yes!" In this reply, down to the word "wager" inclusive, Mademoiselle has been ironically polite and tender; then, as suddenly dashed into the bitterest and most defiant scorn, with her black eyes in one and the same moment very nearly shut, and staringly wide open.

"Now, let us see," says Mr. Tulkinghorn, tapping his chin with the key, and looking imperturbably at her, "how this matter stands."

"Ah! Let us see," Mademoiselle assents, with many angry and tight nods of her head.

"You come here to make a remarkably modest demand, which you have just stated, and it not being conceded, you will come again."

"And again," says Mademoiselle, with more tight and angry nods. "And yet again. And yet again. And many times again. In effect, forever!"

"And not only here, but you will go to Mr. Snagsby's, too, perhaps? That visit not succeeding either, you will go again perhaps?"

"And again," repeats Mademoiselle, cataleptic with determination. "And yet again. And yet again. And many times again. In effect, forever!"

"Very well. Now Mademoiselle Hortense, let me recommend you to take the candle and pick up that money of yours. I think you will find it behind the clerk's partition in the corner yonder."

She merely throws a laugh over her shoulder, and stands her ground with folded arms.

"You will not, eh?"

"No, I will not!"

"So much the poorer you; so much the richer I! Look,

mistress, this is the key of my wine-cellar. It is a large key, but the keys of prisons are larger. In this city, there are houses of correction (where the treadmills are, for women) the gates of which are very strong and heavy, and no doubt the keys too. I am afraid a lady of your spirit and activity would find it an inconvenience to have one of those keys turned upon her for any length of time. What do you think?"

"I think," Mademoiselle replies, without any action, and in a clear obliging voice, "that you are a miserable wretch."

"Probably," returns Mr. Tulkinghorn, quietly blowing his nose. "But I don't ask what you think of myself; I ask what you think of the prison."

"Nothing. What does it matter to me?"

"Why, it matters this much, mistress," says the lawyer, deliberately putting away his handkerchief, and adjusting his frill, "the law is so despotic here, that it interferes to prevent any of our good English citizens from being troubled, even by a lady's visits, against his desire. And, on his complaining that he is so troubled, it takes hold of the troublesome lady, and shuts her up in prison under hard discipline. Turns the key upon her, mistress." Illustrating with the cellar key.

"Truly?" returns Mademoiselle, in the same pleasant voice. "That is droll! But—my faith!—still what does it matter to me?"

"My fair friend," says Mr. Tulkinghorn, "make another visit here, or at Mr. Snagsby's, and you shall learn."

"In that case you will send me to the prison, perhaps?"

"Perhaps."

It would be contradictory for one in Mademoiselle's state of agreeable jocularity to foam at the mouth, otherwise a tigerish expansion thereabouts might look as if a very little more would make her do it.

"In a word, mistress," says Mr. Tulkinghorn, "I am sorry to be unpolite, but if you ever present yourself uninvited here—or there—again, I will give you over to the police. Their gallantry is great, but they carry troublesome people through the streets in an ignominious manner; strapped down on a board, my good wench."

"I will prove you," whispers Mademoiselle, stretching out her hand, "I will try if you dare to do it!"

"And if," pursues the lawyer, without minding her, "I place you in that good condition of being locked up in jail, it will be some time before you find yourself at liberty again."

"I will prove you," repeats Mademoiselle in her former whisper.

"And now," proceeds the lawyer, still without minding her, "you had better go. Think twice before you come here again."

"Think you," she answers, "twice two hundred times!"

"You were dismissed by your lady, you know," Mr. Tulkinghorn observes, following her out upon the staircase, "as the most implacable and unmanageable of women. Now turn over a new leaf, and take warning by what I say to you. For what I say, I mean; and what I threaten, I will do, mistress."

She goes down without answering or looking behind her. When she is gone, he goes down too; and returning with his cobweb-covered bottle, devotes himself to a leisurely enjoyment of its contents: now and then, as he throws his head back in his chair, catching sight of the pertinacious Roman pointing from the ceiling.

XII

CLOSING IN

THE place in Lincolnshire has shut its many eyes again, and the house in town is awake. In Lincolnshire, the Dedlocks of the past doze in their picture-frames, and the low wind murmurs through the long drawing-room as if they were breathing pretty regularly. In town, the Dedlocks of the present rattle in their fire-eyed carriages through the darkness of the night, and the Dedlock Mercuries, with ashes (or hair-powder) on their heads, symptomatic of their great humility, loll away the drowsy mornings in the little windows of the hall. The fashionable world—tremendous orb, nearly five miles round—is in full swing, and the solar system works respectfully at its appointed distances.

Where the throng is thickest, where the lights are brightest, where all the senses are ministered to with the greatest delicacy and refinement, Lady Dedlock is. From the shining heights she has scaled and taken, she is never absent. Though the belief she of old reposed in herself, as one able to reserve whatsoever she would under her mantle of pride, is beaten down; though she has no assurance that what she is to those around her, she will remain another day; it is not in her nature, when envious eyes are looking on, to yield or to droop. They say of her, that she has lately grown more handsome and more haughty. The debilitated cousin says of her that she's beauty nough—tsetup Shopofwomen—but rather larming kind—remindingmanfact—inconvenient woman—who *will* getouofbedandbawthstabishment—Shakespeare.

Mr. Tulkinghorn says nothing; looks nothing. Now, as heretofore, he is to be found in doorways of rooms, with limp white cravat loosely twisted into its old-fashioned tie, receiving patronage from the Peerage, and making no sign. Of all men he is still the last who might be supposed to have any influence upon my Lady. Of all women she is still the last who might be supposed to have any dread of him.

One thing has been much on her mind since their late interview in his turret-room at Chesney Wold. She is now decided, and prepared to throw it off.

Lady Dedlock dines alone in her own room to-day. Sir Leicester is whipped in to the rescue of the Doodle Party, and the discomfiture of the Coodle Faction. Lady Dedlock asks, on sitting down to dinner, still deadly pale (and quite an illustration of the debilitated cousin's text), whether he is gone out? Yes. Whether Mr. Tulkinghorn is gone yet? No. Presently she asks again, is he gone *yet?* No. What is he doing? Mercury thinks he is writing letters in the library. Would my Lady wish to see him? Anything but that.

But he wishes to see my Lady. Within a few more minutes he is reported as sending his respects, and could my Lady please to receive him for a word or two after her dinner? My Lady will receive him now. He comes now, apologizing for intruding, even by her permission, while she is at table. When they are alone, my Lady waves her hand to dispense with such mockeries.

" What do you want, sir?"

" Why, Lady Dedlock," says the lawyer, taking a chair at a little distance from her, and slowly rubbing his rusty legs up and down, up and down, up and down; " I am rather surprised by the course you have taken."

" Indeed? "

" Yes, decidedly. I was not prepared for it. I consider it a departure from our agreement and your promise. It puts us in a new position, Lady Dedlock. I feel myself under the necessity of saying that I don't approve of it."

He stops in his rubbing, and looks at her, with his hands on his knees. Imperturbable and unchangeable as he is, there is still an indefinable freedom in his manner, which is new, and which does not escape this woman's observation.

" I do not quite understand you."

" O yes, you do, I think. I think you do. Come, come, Lady Dedlock, we must not fence and parry now. You know you like this girl."

" Well, sir? "

" And you know—and I know—that you have not sent her away for the reasons you have assigned, but for the purpose of separating her as much as possible from—excuse my mentioning it as a matter of business—any reproach and exposure that impend over yourself."

" Well, sir? "

" Well, Lady Dedlock," returns the lawyer, crossing his legs, and nursing the uppermost knee. " I object to that,

I consider that a dangerous proceeding. I know it to be unnecessary, and calculated to awaken speculation, doubt, rumor, I don't know what, in the house. Besides, it is a violation of our agreement. You were to be exactly what you were before. Whereas, it must be evident to yourself, as it is to me, that you have been this evening very different from what you were before. Why, bless my soul, Lady Dedlock, transparently so!"

"If, sir," she begins, "in my knowledge of my secret——" But he interrupts her.

"Now, Lady Dedlock, this is a matter of business, and in a manner of business the ground cannot be kept too clear. It is no longer your secret. Excuse me. That is just the mistake. It is my secret, in trust for Sir Leicester and the family. If it were your secret, Lady Dedlock, we should not be here, holding this conversation."

"That is very true. If, in my knowledge of *the* secret, I do what I can to spare an innocent girl (especially, remembering your own reference to her when you told my story to the assembled guests at Chesney Wold) from the taint of my impending shame, I act upon a resolution I have taken. Nothing in the world, and no one in the world, could shake it, or could move me." This she says with great deliberation and distinctness, and with no more outward passion than himself. As for him, he methodically discusses his matter of business, as if she were any insensible instrument used in business.

"Really? Then you see, Lady Dedlock," he returns, "you are not to be trusted. You have put the case in a perfectly plain way, and according to the literal fact; and, that being the case, you are not to be trusted."

"Perhaps you may remember that I expressed some anxiety on this same point, when we spoke at night at Chesney Wold?"

"Yes," says Mr. Tulkinghorn, coolly getting up and standing on the hearth. "Yes. I recollect, Lady Dedlock, that you certainly referred to the girl; but that was before we came to our arrangement, and both the letter and the spirit of our arrangement altogether precluded any action on your part, founded upon my discovery. There can be no doubt about that. As to sparing the girl, of what importance or value is she? Spare! Lady Dedlock, here is a family name compromised. One might have supposed that the course was straight on—over everything, neither to the right nor to the left, regardless of all considerations in the way, sparing nothing, treading everything under foot."

She has been looking at the table. She lifts up her eyes, and looks at him. There is a stern expression on her face, and a part of her lower lip is compressed under her teeth. "This woman understands me," Mr. Tulkinghorn thinks, as she lets her glance fall again. "*She* cannot be spared. Why should she spare others?"

For a little while they are silent. Lady Dedlock has eaten no dinner, but has twice or thrice poured out water with a steady hand and drunk it. She rises from table, takes a lounging-chair, and reclines in it, shading her face. There is nothing in her manner to express weakness or excite compassion. It is thoughtful, gloomy, concentrated. "This woman," thinks Mr. Tulkinghorn, standing on the hearth, again a dark object closing up her view, "is a study."

He studies her at his leisure, not speaking for a time. She too studies something at her leisure. She is not the first to speak; appearing indeed so unlikely to be so, though he stood there until midnight, that even he is driven upon breaking silence.

"Lady Dedlock, the most disagreeable part of this business interview remains; but it is business. Our agreement is broken. A lady of your sense and strength of character will be prepared for my now declaring it void, and taking my own course."

"I am quite prepared."

Mr. Tulkinghorn inclines his head. "That is all I have to trouble you with, Lady Dedlock."

She stops him as he is moving out of the room, by asking, " This is the notice I was to receive? I wish not to misapprehend you."

" Not exactly the notice you were to receive, Lady Dedlock, because the contemplated notice supposed the agreement to have been observed. But virtually the same, virtually the same. The difference is merely in a lawyer's mind."

" You intend to give me no other notice? "

" You are right. No."

" Do you contemplate undeceiving Sir Leicester to-night? "

" A home question! " says Mr. Tulkinghorn, with a slight smile, and cautiously shaking his head at the shaded face. " No, not to-night."

" To-morrow? "

" All things considered, I had better decline answering that question, Lady Dedlock. If I were to say I don't know when, exactly, you would not believe me, and it would answer no purpose. It may be to-morrow. I would rather say no more. You are prepared, and I hold out no expectations which circumstances might fail to justify. I wish you good evening."

She removes her hand, turns her pale face towards him as he walks silently to the door, and stops him once again as he is about to open it.

" Do you intend to remain in the house any time? I heard you were writing in the library. Are you going to return there? "

" Only for my hat. I am going home."

She bows her eyes rather than her head, the movement is so slight and curious; and he withdraws. Clear of the room he looks at his watch, but is inclined to doubt it by a minute or thereabouts. There is a splendid clock upon the staircase, famous, as splendid clocks not often are, for its accuracy. " And what do *you* say," Mr. Tulkinghorn inquires, referring to it. " What do you say? "

If it said now, " Don't go home! " What a famous clock, hereafter, if it said to-night of all the nights that it has counted off, to this old man of all the young and old men who ever stood before it, "Don't go home!" With its sharp clear bell, it strikes three-quarters after seven, and ticks on again. "Why, you are worse than I thought you," says Mr. Tulkinghorn, muttering reproof to his watch. "Two minutes wrong? At this rate you won't last my time." What a watch to return good for evil, if it ticked in answer, "Don't go home!"

He passes out into the streets, and walks on, with his hands behind him, under the shadow of the lofty houses, many of whose mysteries, difficulties, mortgages, delicate affairs of all kinds, are treasured up within his old black satin waistcoat. He is in the confidence of the very bricks and mortar. The high chimney-stacks telegraph family secrets to him. Yet there is not a voice in a mile of them to whisper, "Don't go home!"

Through the stir and motion of the commoner streets; through the roar and jar of many vehicles, many feet, many voices; with the blazing shop-lights lighting him on, the west wind blowing him on, and the crowd pressing him on; he is pitilessly urged upon his way, and nothing meets him, murmuring, "Don't go home!" Arrived at last in his dull room, to light his candles, and look round and up, and see the Roman pointing from the ceiling, there is no new significance in the Roman's hand to-night, or in the flutter of the attendant groups, to give him the late warning, "Don't come here!"

It is a moonlight night: but the moon, being past the full, is only now rising over the great wilderness of London. The stars are shining as they shone above the turret-leads at Chesney Wold. This woman, as he has of late been so accustomed to call her, looks out upon them. Her soul is turbulent within her; she is sick at heart, and restless. The large rooms are too cramped and close. She cannot endure their restraint, and will walk alone in a neighboring garden.

Too capricious and imperious in all she does, to be the cause of much surprise in those about her as to anything she does, this woman, loosely muffled, goes out into the moonlight. Mercury attends with the key. Having opened the garden-gate, he delivers the key into his Lady's hands at her request, and is bidden to go back. She will walk there some time, to ease her aching head. She may be an hour; she may be more. She needs no further escort. The gate shuts upon its spring with a clash, and he leaves her, passing on into the dark shades of some trees.

A fine night, and a bright large moon, and multitudes of stars. Mr. Tulkinghorn, in repairing to his cellar, and in opening and shutting those resounding doors, has to cross a little prison-like yard. He looks up casually, thinking what a fine night, what a bright large moon, what multitudes of stars! A quiet night, too.

A very quiet night. When the moon shines very brilliantly, a solitude and stillness seem to proceed from her, that influence even crowded places full of life. Not only is it a still night on dusty high-roads and on hill-summits, whence a wide expanse of country may be seen in repose, quieter and quieter as it spreads away into a fringe of trees against the sky, with the gray ghost of a bloom upon them; not only is it a still night in gardens and in woods, and on the river where the water-meadows are fresh and green, and the stream sparkles on among pleasant islands, murmuring weirs, and whispering rushes; not only does the stillness attend it as it flows where houses cluster thick, where many bridges are reflected in it, where wharves and shipping make it black and awful, where it winds from these disfigurements through marshes whose grim beacons stand like skeletons washed ashore, where it expands through the bolder region of rising grounds, rich in cornfield, wind-mill, and steeple, and where it mingles with the ever-heaving sea; not only is it a still night on the deep, and on the shore where the watcher stands to see the ship with her spread wings cross the path of light that appears to be presented to only him; but even on this stranger's wilderness of London there is some rest. Its steeples and towers, and its one great dome, grow more ethereal; its smoky house-tops lose their grossness, in the pale effulgence; the noises that arise from the streets are fewer and are softened, and the footsteps on the pavements pass more tranquilly away. In these fields of Mr. Tulkinghorn's inhabiting, where the shepherds play on Chancery pipes that have no stop, and keep their sheep in the fold by hook and by crook until they have shorn them exceedingly close, every noise is merged, this moonlight night, into a distant ringing hum, as if the city were a vast glass, vibrating.

What's that? Who fired a gun or pistol? Where was it? The few foot-passengers start, stop, and stare about them. Some windows and doors are opened, and people come out to look. It was a loud report, and echoed and rattled heavily. It shook one house, or so a man says who was passing. It has aroused all the dogs in the neighborhood, who bark vehemently. Terrified cats scamper across the road. While the dogs are yet barking and howling—there is one dog howling like a demon—the church-clocks, as if they were startled too, begin to strike. The hum from the streets, likewise, seems to swell into a shout. But it is soon over. Before the last clock begins to strike ten, there is a lull. When it has ceased, the fine night, the bright large moon, and multitudes of stars, are left at peace again.

Has Mr. Tulkinghorn been disturbed? His windows are dark and quiet, and his door is shut. It must be something unusual indeed, to bring him out of his shell. Nothing is heard of him, nothing is seen of him. What power of cannon might it take to shake that rusty old man out of his immovable composure?

For many years, the persistent Roman has been pointing, with no particular meaning, from that ceiling. It is not likely that he has any new meaning in him to-night. Once pointing, always pointing—like any Roman, or even Briton, with a single idea. There he is, no doubt, in his impossible attitude, pointing, unavailingly, all night long. Moonlight, darkness, dawn, sunrise, day. There he is still, eagerly pointing, and no one minds him.

But, a little after the coming of the day, come people to

clean the rooms. And either the Roman has some new meaning in him, not expressed before, or the foremost of them goes wild; for, looking up at his outstretched hand, and looking down at what is below it, that person shrieks and flies. The others, looking in as the first one looked, shriek and fly too, and there is an alarm in the street.

What does it mean? No light is admitted into the darkened chamber, and people unaccustomed to it, enter, and treading softly, but heavily, carry a weight into the bedroom, and lay it down. There is whispering and wondering all day, strict search of every corner, careful tracing of steps, and careful noting of the disposition of every article of furniture. All eyes look up at the Roman, and all voices murmur, " If he could only tell what he saw! "

He is pointing at a table, with a bottle (nearly full of wine) and a glass upon it, and two candles that were blown out suddenly, soon after being lighted. He is pointing at an empty chair, and at a stain upon the ground before it that might be almost covered with a hand. These objects lie directly within his range. An excited imagination might suppose that there was something in them so terrific, as to drive the rest of the composition, not only the attendant big-legged boys, but the clouds and flowers and pillars too—in short, the very body and soul of Allegory, and all the brains it has—stark mad. It happens surely, that every one who comes into the darkened room and looks at these things, looks up at the Roman, and that he is invested in all eyes with mystery and awe, as if he were a paralyzed dumb witness.

So, it shall happen surely, through many years to come, that ghostly stories shall be told of the stain upon the floor, so easy to be covered, so hard to be got out; and that the Roman, pointing from the ceiling, shall point, so long as dust and damp and spiders spare him, with far greater significance than he ever had in Mr. Tulkinghorn's time, and with a deadly meaning. For, Mr. Tulkinghorn's time is over for evermore; and the Roman pointed at the murderous hand uplifted against his life, and pointed helplessly at him, from night to morning, lying face downward on the floor, shot through the heart.

XIII

THE TRACK

MR. BUCKET and his fat forefinger are much in consultation together under existing circumstances. When Mr. Bucket has a matter of this pressing interest under his consideration, the fat forefinger seems to rise to the dignity of a familiar demon. He puts it to his ears, and it whispers information; he puts it to his lips, and it enjoins him to secrecy; he rubs it over his nose, and it sharpens his scent; he shakes it before a guilty man, and it charms him to his destruction. The Augurs of the Detective Temple invariably predict, that when Mr. Bucket and that finger are in much conference, a terrible avenger will be heard of before long.

Otherwise mildly studious in his observation of human nature, on the whole a benignant philosopher not disposed to be severe upon the follies of mankind, Mr. Bucket pervades a vast number of houses, and strolls about an infinity of streets: to outward appearance rather languishing for want of an object. He is in the friendliest condition towards his species, and will drink with most of them. He is free with his money, affable in his manners, innocent in his conversation—but, through the placid stream of his life, there glides an under-current of forefinger.

Time and place cannot bind Mr. Bucket. Like man in the abstract, he is here to-day and gone to-morrow—but, very unlike man indeed, he is here again the next day. This evening he will be casually looking into the iron extinguishers at the door of Sir Leicester Dedlock's house in town: and to-morrow morning he will be walking on the leads at Chesney Wold, where erst the old man walked whose ghost is propitiated with a hundred guineas. Drawers, desks, pockets, all things belonging to him, Mr. Bucket

133

examines. A few hours afterwards, he and the Roman will be alone together, comparing forefingers.

It is likely that these occupations are irreconcilable with home enjoyment, but it is certain that Mr. Bucket at present does not go home. Though in general he highly appreciates the society of Mrs. Bucket—a lady of a natural detective genius, which, if it had been improved by professional exercise, might have done great things, but which has paused at the level of a clever amateur—he holds himself aloof from that dear solace. Mrs. Bucket is dependent on their lodger (fortunately an amiable lady in whom she takes an interest) for companionship and conversation.

A great crowd assembles in Lincoln's Inn Fields on the day of the funeral. Sir Leicester Dedlock attends the ceremony in person; strictly speaking, there are only three other human followers, that is to say, Lord Doodle, William Buffy, and the debilitated cousin (thrown in as a makeweight), but the amount of inconsolable carriages is immense. The Peerage contributes more four-wheeled affliction than has ever been seen in that neighborhood. Such is the assemblage of armorial bearings on coach panels, that the Heralds' College might be supposed to have lost its father and mother at a blow. The Duke of Foodle sends a splendid pile of dust and ashes, with silver wheelboxes, patent axles, all the last improvements, and three bereaved worms, six feet high, holding on behind, in a bunch of woe. All the state coachmen in London seem plunged into mourning; and if that dead old man of the rusty garb be not beyond a taste in horseflesh (which appears impossible), it must be highly gratified this day.

Quiet among the undertakers and the equipages, and the calves of so many legs all steeped in grief, Mr. Bucket sits concealed in one of the inconsolable carriages, and at his ease surveys the crowd through the lattice blinds. He has a keen eye for a crowd—as for what not?—and looking here and there, now from this side of the carriage, now from the other, now up at the house windows, now along the people's heads, nothing escapes him.

"And there you are, my partner, eh?" says Mr. Bucket to himself, apostrophizing Mrs. Bucket, stationed, by his favor, on the steps of the deceased's house. "And so you are! And so you are! And very well indeed you are looking, Mrs. Bucket!"

The procession has not started yet, but is waiting for the cause of its assemblage to be brought out. Mr. Bucket, in the foremost emblazoned carriage, uses his two fat forefingers to hold the lattice a hair's breadth open while he looks.

And it says a great deal for his attachment, as a husband, that he is still occupied with Mrs. B. "There you are, my partner, eh?" he murmuringly repeats. "And our lodger with you. I'm taking notice of you, Mrs. Bucket; I hope you're all right in your health, my dear!"

Not another word does Mr. Bucket say; but sits with most attentive eyes until the sacked depository of noble secrets is brought down—— Where are all those secrets now? Does he keep them yet? Did they fly with him on that sudden journey?—and until the procession moves, and Mr. Bucket's view is changed. After which he composes himself for an easy ride; and takes note of the fittings of the carriage, in case he should ever find such knowledge useful.

Contrast enough between Mr. Tulkinghorn shut up in his dark carriage, and Mr. Bucket shut up in *his*. Between the immeasurable track of space beyond the little wound that has thrown the one into the fixed sleep which jolts so heavily over the stones of the streets, and the narrow track of blood which keeps the other in the watchful state expressed in every hair of his head! But it is all one to both; neither is troubled about that.

Mr. Bucket sits out the procession in his own easy manner, and glides from the carriage when the opportunity he has settled with himself arrives. He makes for Sir Leicester Dedlock's, which is at present a sort of home to him, where he comes and goes as he likes at all hours, where he is always welcome and made much of, where he knows the whole establishment, and walks in an atmosphere of mysterious greatness.

No knocking or ringing for Mr. Bucket. He has caused himself to be provided with a key, and can pass at his pleasure. As he is crossing the hall, Mercury informs him, " Here's another letter for you, Mr. Bucket, come by post," and gives it to him.

" Another one, eh? " says Mr. Bucket.

If Mercury should chance to be possessed by any lingering curiosity as to Mr. Bucket's letters, that wary person is not the man to gratify it. Mr. Bucket looks at him as if his face were a vista of some miles in length, and he were leisurely contemplating the same.

" Do you happen to carry a box? " says Mr. Bucket.

Unfortunately Mercury is no snuff-taker.

" Coud you fetch me a pinch from anywheres? " says Mr. Bucket. " Thankee. It don't matter what it is; I'm not particular as to the kind. Thankee! "

Having leisurely helped himself from a canister borrowed from somebody downstairs for the purpose, and having made a considerable show of tasting it, first with one side of his nose and then with the other, Mr. Bucket, with much deliberation, pronounces it of the right sort, and goes on, letter in hand.

Now, although Mr. Bucket walks upstairs to the little library within the larger one, with the face of a man who receives some scores of letters every day, it happens that much correspondence is not incidental to his life. He is no great scribe; rather handling his pen like the pocket-staff he carries about with him always convenient to his grasp; and discourages correspondence with himself in others, as being too artless and direct a way of doing delicate business. Further, he often sees damaging letters produced in evidence, and has occasion to reflect that it was a green thing to write them. For these reasons he has very little to do with letters, either as sender or receiver. And yet he has received a round half-dozen within the last twenty-four hours.

"And this," says Mr. Bucket, spreading it out on the table, "is in the same hand, and consists of the same two words."

What two words?

He turns the key in the door, ungirdles his black pocket-book (book of fate to many), lays another letter by it, and reads, boldly written in each, "LADY DEDLOCK."

"Yes, yes," says Mr. Bucket. "But I could have made the money without this anonymous information."

Having put the letters in his book of fate, and girdling it up again, he unlocks the door just in time to admit his dinner, which is brought upon a goodly tray, with a decanter of sherry. Mr. Bucket frequently observes, in friendly circles where there is no restraint, that he likes a toothful of your fine old brown East Inder sherry better than anything you can offer him. Consequently he fills and empties his glass, with a smack of his lips; and is proceeding with his refreshment, when an idea enters his mind.

Mr. Bucket softly opens the door of communication between that room and the next, and looks in. The library is deserted, and the fire is sinking low. Mr. Bucket's eye, after taking a pigeon-flight around the room, alights upon a table where letters are usually put as they arrive. Several letters for Sir Leicester are upon it. Mr. Bucket draws near and examines the directions. "No," he says, "there's none in that hand. It's only me as is written to. I can break it to Sir Leicester Dedlock, Baronet, to-morrow."

With that he returns to finish his dinner with a good appetite; and after a light nap, is summoned into the drawing-room. Sir Leicester has received him there these several evenings past, to know whether he has anything to report. The debilitated cousin (much exhausted by the funeral), and Volumnia, are in attendance.

Mr. Bucket makes three distinctly different bows to these three people. A bow of homage to Sir Leicester, a bow of gallantry to Volumnia, and a bow of recognition to the debilitated cousin; to whom it airily says, "You are a swell about town, and you know me, and I know you." Having distributed these little specimens of his tact, Mr. Bucket rubs his hands.

" Have you anything new to communicate, officer? " inquires Sir Leicester. " Do you wish to hold any conversation with me in private? "

" Why—not to night, Sir Leicester Dedlock, Baronet."

" Because my time," pursues Sir Leicester, " is wholly at your disposal, with a view to the vindication of the outraged majesty of the law."

Mr. Bucket coughs and glances at Volumnia, rouged and necklaced, as though he would respectfully observe, " I do assure you, you're a pretty creetur. I've seen hundreds worse-looking at your time of life, I have indeed."

The fair Volumnia, not quite unconscious perhaps of the humanizing influence of her charms, pauses in the writing of cocked-hat notes, and meditatively adjusts the pearl necklace. Mr. Bucket prices that decoration in his mind, and thinks it as likely as not that Volumnia is writing poetry.

" If I have not," pursues Sir Leicester, " in the most emphatic manner, adjured you, officer, to exercise your utmost skill in this atrocious case, I particularly desire to take the present opportunity of rectifying any omission I may have made. Let no expense be a consideration. I am prepared to defray all charges. You can incur none, in pursuit of the object you have undertaken, that I shall hesitate for a moment to bear."

Mr. Bucket made Sir Leicester's bow again, as a response to this liberality.

" My mind," Sir Leicester adds, with generous warmth, " has not, as may be easily supposed, recovered its tone since the late diabolical occurrence. It is not likely ever to recover its tone. But it is full of indignation to-night, after undergoing the ordeal of consigning to the tomb the remains of a faithful, a zealous, a devoted adherent."

Sir Leicester's voice trembles, and his gray hair stirs upon his head. Tears are in his eyes; the best part of his nature is aroused.

" I declare," he says, " I solemnly declare that until this

crime is discovered and, in the course of justice, punished, I almost feel as if there were a stain upon my name. A gentleman who has devoted a large portion of his life to me, a gentleman who has devoted the last day of his life to me, a gentleman who has constantly sat at my table and slept under my roof, goes from my house to his own, and is struck down within an hour of his leaving my house. I cannot say but that he may have been followed from my house, watched at my house, even first marked because of his association with my house—which may have suggested his possessing greater wealth, and being altogether of greater importance than his own retiring demeanor would have indicated. If I cannot, with my means and influence, and my position, bring all the perpetrators of such a crime to light, I fail in the assertion of my respect for that gentleman's memory, and of my fidelity towards one who was ever faithful to me."

While he makes this protestation with great emotion and earnestness, looking round the room as if he were addressing an assembly, Mr. Bucket glances at him with an observant gravity in which there might be, but for the audacity of the thought, a touch of compassion.

"The ceremony of to-day," continues Sir Leicester, "strikingly illustrative of the respect in which my deceased friend;" he lays a stress upon the word, for death levels all distinction; "was held by the flower of the land, has, I say, aggravated the shock I have received from this most horrible and audacious crime. If it were my brother who had committed it, I would not spare him."

Mr. Bucket looks very grave. Volumnia remarks of the deceased that he was the trustiest and dearest person!

"You must feel it as a deprivation to you, miss," replied Mr. Bucket, soothingly, "no doubt. He was calculated to *be* a deprivation, I'm sure he was."

Volumnia gives Mr. Bucket to understand, in reply, that her sensitive mind is fully made up never to get the better of it as long as she lives; that her nerves are unstrung for ever; and that she has not the least expectation of ever smiling again. Meanwhile she folds up a cocked hat for that redoubtable old general at Bath, descriptive of her melancholy condition.

"It gives a start to a delicate female," says Mr. Bucket, sympathetically, "but it'll wear off."

Volumnia wishes of all things to know what is doing? Whether they are going to convict, or whatever it is, that dreadful soldier? Whether he had any accomplices, or whatever the thing is called in the law? And a great deal more to the like artless purpose.

"Why, you see, miss," returns Mr. Bucket, bringing the finger into persuasive action—and such is his natural gallantry, that he had almost said, my dear; "it ain't easy to answer those questions at the present moment. Not at the present moment. I've kept myself on this case, Sir Leicester Dedlock, Baronet," whom Mr. Bucket takes into the conversation in right of his importance, "morning, noon, and night. But for a glass or two of sherry, I don't think I could have had my mind so much upon the stretch as it has been. I *could* answer your question, miss, but duty forbids it. Sir Leicester Dedlock, Baronet, will very soon be made acquainted with all that has been traced. And I hope that he may find it;" Mr. Bucket again looks grave; "to his satisfaction."

The debilitated cousin only hopes some fler'll be executed—zample. Thinks more interest's wanted—get man hanged presentime—than get man place ten thousand a year. Hasn't a doubt—zample—far better hang wrong fler than no fler.

"*You* know life, you know, sir," says Mr. Bucket, with a complimentary twinkle of his eye and crook of his finger, "and you can confirm what I've mentioned to this lady. *You* don't want to be told, that, from information I have received, I have gone to work. You're up to what a lady can't be expected to be up to. Lord! especially in your elevated station of society, miss," says Mr. Bucket, quite reddening at another narrow escape from my dear.

"The officer, Volumnia," observes Sir Leicester, "is faithful to his duty, and perfectly right."

Mr. Bucket murmurs, "Glad to have the honor o' your approbation, Sir Leicester Dedlock, Baronet."

"In fact, Volumnia," proceeds Sir Leicester, "it is not holding up a good model for imitation, to ask the officer any such questions as you have put to him. He is the best judge of his own responsibility; he acts upon his responsibility. And it does not become us, who assist in making the laws, to impede or interfere with those who carry them into execution. Or," says Sir Leicester, somewhat sternly, for Volumnia was going to cut in before he had rounded his sentence; "or who vindicate their outraged majesty."

Volumnia with all humility explains that she has not merely the plea of curiosity to urge (in common with the giddy youth of her sex in general), but that she is perfectly dying with regret and interest for the darling man whose loss they all deplore.

"Very well, Volumnia," returns Sir Leicester. "Then you cannot be too discreet."

Mr. Bucket takes the opportunity of a pause to be heard again.

"Sir Leicester Dedlock, Baronet, I have no objections to telling this lady, with your leave and among ourselves, that I look upon the case as pretty well complete. It is a beautiful case—a beautiful case—and what little is wanting to complete it, I expect to be able to supply in a few hours."

"I am very glad indeed to hear it," says Sir Leicester. "Highly creditable to you."

"Sir Leicester Dedlock, Baronet," returns Mr. Bucket, very seriously, "I hope it may at one and the same time do me credit, and prove satisfactory to all. When I depict it as a beautiful case, you see, miss," Mr. Bucket goes on, glancing gravely at Sir Leicester, "I mean from my point of view. As considered from other points of view, such cases will always involve more or less unpleasantness. Very strange things comes to our knowledge in families, miss; bless your heart, what you would think to be phenomenons, quite."

Volumnia, with her innocent little scream, supposes so.

"Aye, and even in gen-teel families, in high families, in great families," says Mr. Bucket, again gravely eying Sir Leicester aside. "I have had the honor of being employed in high families before; and you have no idea—come, I'll go so far as to say not even *you* have any idea, sir," this to the debilitated cousin, "what games goes on!"

The cousin, who has been casting sofa-pillows on his head, in a prostration of boredom, yawns, "Vayli"—being the used-up for "very likely."

Sir Leicester, deeming it time to dismiss the officer, here majestically interposes with the words, "Very good. Thank you!" and also with a wave of his hand, implying not only that there is an end of the discourse, but that if high families fall into low habits they must take the consequences. "You will not forget, officer," he adds, with condescension, "that I am at your disposal when you please."

Mr. Bucket (still grave) inquires if to-morrow morning, now, would suit, in case he should be as for'ard as he expects to be? Sir Leicester replies, "All times are alike to me." Mr. Bucket makes his three bows, and is withdrawing, when a forgotten point occurs to him.

"Might I ask, by-the-bye," he says, in a low voice, cautiously returning, "who posted the reward-bill on the staircase."

"*I* ordered it to be put up there," replies Sir Leicester.

"Would it be considered a liberty, Sir Leicester Dedlock, Baronet, if I was to ask you why?"

"Not at all. I chose it as a conspicuous part of the house. I think it cannot be too prominently kept before the whole establishment. I wish my people to be impressed with the enormity of the crime, the determination to punish it, and the hopelessness of escape. At the same time, officer, if you in your better knowledge of the subject see any objection——"

Mr. Bucket sees none now; the bill having been put up,

had better not be taken down. Repeating his three bows he withdraws: closing the door on Volumnia's little scream, which is a preliminary to her remarking that that charmingly horrible person is a perfect Blue Chamber.

In his fondness for society. and his adaptability to all grades, Mr. Bucket is presently standing before the hall-fire—bright and warm on the early winter night—admiring Mercury.

" Why, you're six foot two, I suppose? " says Mr. Bucket.

" Three," says Mercury.

" Are you so much? But then, you see, you're broad in proportion, and don't look it. You're not one of the weak-legged ones, you ain't. Was you ever modeled now? " Mr. Bucket asks, conveying the expression of an artist into the turn of his eye and head.

Mercury never was modeled.

" Then you ought to be, you know," says Mr. Bucket; " and a friend of mine that you'll hear of one day as a Royal Academy sculptor, would stand something handsome to make a drawing of your proportions for the marble. My Lady's out, ain't she? "

" Out to dinner."

" Goes out pretty well every day, don't she? "

" Yes."

" Not to be wondered at! " says Mr. Bucket. " Such a fine woman as her, so handsome and so graceful and so elegant, is like a fresh lemon on a dinner-table, ornamental wherever she goes. Was your father in the same way of life as yourself? "

Answer in the negative.

" Mine was," says Mr. Bucket. " My father was first a page, then a footman, then a butler, then a steward, then an innkeeper. Lived universally respected, and died lamented. Said with his last breath that he considered service the most honorable part of his career, and so it was. I've a brother in the service, *and* a brother-in-law. My Lady a good temper? "

Mercury replies, " As good as you can expect."

"Ah!" says Mr. Bucket, "a little spoilt? A little capricious? Lord! What can you anticipate when they are so handsome as that? And we like 'em all the better for it, don't we?"

Mercury, with his hands in the pockets of his bright peach-blossom small-clothes, stretches his symmetrical silk legs with the air of a man of gallantry, and can't deny it. Come the roll of wheels, and a violent ringing at the bell. "Talk of the angels," says Mr. Bucket. "Here she is!"

The doors are thrown open, and she passes through the hall. Still very pale, she is dressed in slight mourning, and wears two beautiful bracelets. Either their beauty, or the beauty of her arms, is particularly attractive to Mr. Bucket. He looks at them with an eager eye, and rattles something in his pockets—halfpence perhaps.

Noticing him at his distance, she turns an inquiring look on the other Mercury who has brought her home.

"Mr. Bucket, my Lady."

Mr. Bucket makes a leg, and comes forward, passing his familiar demon over the region of his mouth.

"Are you waiting to see Sir Leicester?"

"No, my Lady, I've seen him!"

"Have you anything to say to me?"

"Not just at present, my Lady."

"Have you made any new discoveries?"

"A few, my Lady."

This is merely in passing. She scarcely makes a stop, and sweeps upstairs alone. Mr. Bucket, moving towards the staircase foot, watches her as she goes up the steps the old man came down to his grave; past murderous groups of statuary, repeated with their shadowy weapons on the wall; past the printed bill, which she looks at going by; out of view.

"She's a lovely woman, too, she really is," says Mr. Bucket, coming back to Mercury. "Don't look quite healthy though."

Is not quite healthy, Mercury informs him. Suffers much from headaches.

Really? That's a pity! Walking Mr. Bucket would recommend for that. Well, she tries walking, Mercury rejoins. Walks sometimes for two hours, when she has them bad. By night too.

"Are you sure you're quite so much as six foot three?" asks Mr. Bucket, "begging your pardon for interrupting you a moment?"

Not a doubt about it.

"You're so well put together that I shouldn't have thought it. But the household troops, though considered fine men, are built so straggling.—Walks by night, does she? When it's moonlight, though?"

O yes. When it's moonlight! Of course. O, of course! Conversational and acquiescent on both sides.

"I suppose you ain't in the habit of walking yourself?" says Mr. Bucket. "Not much time for it, I should say?"

Besides which, Mercury don't like it. Prefers carriage exercise.

"To be sure," says Mr. Bucket. "That makes a difference. Now I think of it," says Mr. Bucket, warming his hands, and looking pleasantly at the blaze, "she went out walking, the very night of this business."

"To be sure she did! I let her into the garden over the way."

"And left her there. Certainly you did. I saw you doing it."

"I didn't see *you*," says Mercury.

"I was rather in a hurry," returns Mr. Bucket, "for I was going to visit a aunt of mine that lives at Chelsea—next door but two to the old original Bun House—ninety year old the old lady is, a single woman, and got a little property. Yes, I chanced to be passing at the time. Let's see. What time might it be? It wasn't ten."

"Half-past nine."

"You're right. So it was. And if I don't deceive myself, my Lady was muffled in a loose black mantle, with a deep fringe to it?"

"Of course she was."

Of course she was. Mr. Bucket must return to a little work he has to get on with upstairs; but he must shake hands with Mercury, in acknowledgment of his agreeable conversation, and will he—this is all he asks—will he, when he has a leisure half-hour, think of bestowing it on that Royal Academy sculptor, for the advantage of both parties?

XIV

SPRINGING A MINE

REFRESHED by sleep, Mr. Bucket rises betimes in the morning, and prepares for a field-day. Smartened up by the aid of a clean shirt, and a wet hairbrush, with which instrument, on occasions of ceremony, he lubricates such thin locks as remain to him after his life of severe study, Mr. Bucket lays in a breakfast of two mutton chops as a foundation to work upon, together with tea, eggs, toast, and marmalade on a corresponding scale. Having much enjoyed these strengthening matters, and having held subtle conference with his familiar demon, he confidently instructs Mercury " just to mention quietly to Sir Leicester Dedlock, Baronet, that whenever he's ready for me, I'm ready for him." A gracious message being returned that Sir Leicester will expedite his dressing and join Mr. Bucket in the library within ten minutes, Mr. Bucket repairs to that apartment; and stands before the fire, with his finger on his chin, looking at the blazing coals.

Thoughtful Mr. Bucket is; as a man may be, with weighty work to do; but composed, sure, confident. From the expression of his face, he might be a famous whist-player for a large stake—say a hundred guineas certain —with the game in his hand, but with a high reputation involved in his playing his hand out to the last card, in a masterly way. Not in the least anxious or disturbed is Mr. Bucket when Sir Leicester appears; but he eyes the baronet aside as he comes slowly to his easy-chair, with that observant gravity of yesterday, in which there might have been, but for the audacity of the idea, a touch of compassion.

"I am sorry to have kept you waiting, officer, but I am rather later than my usual hour this morning. I am not well. The agitation, and the indignation from which I have recently suffered, have been too much for me. I am subject to—gout;" Sir Leicester was going to say indisposition, and would have said it to anybody else, but Mr. Bucket palpably knows all about it; "and recent circumstances have brought it on."

As he takes his seat with some difficulty, and with an air of pain, Mr. Bucket draws a little nearer, standing with one of his large hands on the library-table.

"I am not aware, officer," Sir Leicester observes, raising his eyes to his face, "whether you wish us to be alone; but that is entirely as you please. If you do, well and good. If not, Miss Dedlock would be interested——"

"Why, Sir Leicester Dedlock, Baronet," returns Mr. Bucket, with his head persuasively on one side, and his forefinger pendant at one ear like an ear-ring, "we can't be too private just at present. You will presently see that we can't be too private. A lady, under the circumstances, and especially in Miss Dedlock's elevated station of society, can't but be agreeable to me; but speaking without a view to myself, I will take the liberty of assuring you that *I* know we can't be too private."

"That is enough."

"So much so, Sir Leicester Dedlock, Baronet," Mr. Bucket resumes, "that I was on the point of asking your permission to turn the key in the door."

"By all means." Mr. Bucket skillfully and softly takes that precaution; stooping on his knee for a moment, from mere force of habit, so to adjust the key in the lock as that no one shall peep in from the outer side.

"Sir Leicester Dedlock, Baronet, I mentioned yesterday evening, that I wanted but a very little to complete this case. I have now completed it, and collected proof against the person who did this crime."

"Against the soldier?"

"No, Sir Leicester Dedlock; not the soldier."

Sir Leicester looks astounded, and inquires, "Is the man in custody?"

Mr. Bucket tells him, after a pause, "It was a woman."

Sir Leicester leans back in his chair, and breathlessly ejaculates, "Good Heaven!"

"Now, Sir Leicester Dedlock, Baronet," Mr. Bucket begins, standing over him with one hand spread out on the library-table, and the forefinger of the other in impressive use, "it's my duty to prepare you for a train of circumstances that may, and I go so far as to say that will, give you a shock. But, Sir Leicester Dedlock, Baronet, you are a gentleman; and I know what a gentleman is, and what a gentleman is capable of. A gentleman can bear a shock, when it must come, boldly and steadily. A gentleman can make up his mind to stand up against almost any blow. Why, take yourself, Sir Leicester Dedlock, Baronet. If there's a blow to be inflicted on you, you naturally think of your family. You ask yourself, how would all them ancestors of yours, away to Julius Cæsar—not to go beyond him at present—have borne that blow; you remember scores of them that would have borne it well; and you bear it well on their accounts, and to maintain the family credit. That's the way you argue, and that's the way you act, Sir Leicester Dedlock, Baronet."

Sir Leicester, leaning back in his chair, and grasping the elbows, sits looking at him with a stony face.

"Now, Sir Leicester Dedlock," proceeds Mr. Bucket, "thus preparing you, let me beg of you not to trouble your mind, for a moment, as to anything having come to *my* knowledge. I know so much about so many characters, high and low, that a piece of information more or less, don't signify a straw. I don't suppose there's a move on the board that would surprise *me;* and as to this or that move having taken place, why, my knowing it is no odds at all; any possible move whatever (provided it's in a wrong direction) being a probable move according to my experience. Therefore, what I say to you, Sir Leicester Dedlock, Baronet, is, don't you go and let yourself be put out of the way, because of my knowing anything of your family affairs."

"I thank you for your preparation," returns Sir Leicester, after a silence, without moving hand, foot, or feature; "which I hope is not necessary, though I give it credit for being well intended. Be so good as to go on. Also;" Sir Leicester seems to shrink in the shadow of his figure; "also take a seat, if you have no objection."

None at all. Mr. Bucket brings a chair, and diminishes his shadow. "Now, Sir Leicester Dedlock, Baronet, with this short preface I come to the point. Lady Dedlock——"

Sir Leicester raises himself in his seat, and stares at him fiercely. Mr. Bucket brings the finger into play as an emollient.

"Lady Dedlock, you see she's universally admired. That's what her Ladyship is; she's universally admired," says Mr. Bucket.

"I would greatly prefer, officer," Sir Leicester returns, stiffly, "my Lady's name being entirely omitted from this discussion."

"So would I, Sir Leicester Dedlock, Baronet, but—it's impossible."

"Impossible?"

Mr. Bucket shakes his relentless head.

"Sir Leicester Dedlock, Baronet, it's altogether impossible. What I have got to say is about her Ladyship. She is the pivot it all turns on."

"Officer," retorts Sir Leicester, with a fiery eye, and a quivering lip, "you know your duty. Do your duty; but be careful not to overstep it. I would not suffer it. I would not endure it. You bring my Lady's name into this communication, upon your responsibility—upon your responsibility. My Lady's name is not a name for common persons to trifle with!"

"Sir Leicester Dedlock, Baronet, I say what I must say; and no more."

"I hope it may prove so. Very well. Go on. Go on, sir!"

Glancing at the angry eyes which now avoid him, and at the angry figure trembling from head to foot, yet striving to be still, Mr. Bucket feels his way with his forefinger, and in a low voice proceeds.

"Sir Leicester Dedlock, Baronet, it becomes my duty to tell you that the deceased Mr. Tulkinghorn long entertained mistrust and suspicions of Lady Dedlock."

"If he had dared to breathe them to me, sir—which he never did—I would have killed him myself!" exclaims Sir Leicester, striking his hand upon the table. But in the very heat and fury of the act, he stops, fixed by the knowing eyes of Mr. Bucket, whose forefinger is slowly going, and who, with mingled confidence and patience, shakes his head.

"Sir Leicester Dedlock, the deceased Mr. Tulkinghorn was deep and close; and what he fully had in his mind in the very beginning, I can't take upon myself to say. But I know from his lips, that he long ago suspected Lady Dedlock of having discovered, through the sight of some handwriting—in this very house, and when you yourself, Sir Leicester Dedlock, were present—the existence, in great poverty, of a certain person, who had been her lover before you courted her, and who ought to have been her husband;" Mr. Bucket stops, and deliberately repeats, "ought to have been her husband; not a doubt about it. I know from his lips, that when that person soon afterwards died, he suspected Lady Dedlock of visiting his wretched lodging, and his wretched grave alone, and in secret. I know from my own inquiries, and through my eyes and ears, that Lady Dedlock did make such visit, in the dress of her own maid; for the deceased Mr. Tulkinghorn employed me to reckon up her Ladyship—if you'll excuse my making use of the term we commonly employ—and I reckoned her up, so far, completely. I confronted the maid, in the chambers in Lincoln's Inn Fields, with a witness who had been Lady Dedlock's guide; and there couldn't be the shadow of a doubt that she had worn the young woman's dress, unknown to her. Sir Leicester Dedlock, Baronet, I did endeavor to pave the way a little towards these unpleasant disclosures, yesterday, by saying that very strange things happened even in high families sometimes. All this, and more, has happened in your own family, and to and through your own Lady. It is my belief that the deceased Mr. Tulkinghorn followed up these inquiries to the hour of his death; and that he and Lady Dedlock even had bad blood between them upon the matter that very night. Now, only you put that to Lady Dedlock, Sir Leicester Dedlock, Baronet; and ask her Ladyship whether, even after he had left here, she didn't go down to his chambers with the intention of saying something further to him, dressed in a loose black mantle with a deep fringe to it."

Sir Leicester sits like a statue, gazing at the cruel finger that is probing the life-blood of his heart.

"You put that to her Ladyship, Sir Leicester Dedlock, Baronet, from me, Inspector Bucket of the Detective. And if her Ladyship makes any difficulty about admitting of it, you tell her that it's no use; that Inspector Bucket knows it, and knows that she passed the soldier as you called him (though he's not in the army now), and knows that she knows she passed him, on the staircase. Now, Sir Leicester Dedlock, Baronet, why do I relate all this?"

Sir Leicester, who has covered his face with his hands, uttering a single groan, requests him to pause for a moment. By-and-by he takes his hands away; and so preserves his dignity and outward calmness, though there is no more color in his face than in his white hair, that Mr. Bucket is a little awed by him. Something frozen and fixed is upon his manner, over and above its usual shell of haughtiness; and Mr. Bucket soon detects an unusual slowness in his speech, with now and then a curious trouble in beginning, which occasions him to utter inarticulate sounds. With such sounds, he now breaks silence; soon, however, controlling himself to say, that he does not comprehend why a gentleman so faithful and zealous as the late Mr. Tulkinghorn should have communicated to him nothing of this painful, this distressing, this unlooked-for, this overwhelming, this incredible intelligence.

"Again, Sir Leicester Dedlock, Baronet," returns Mr. Bucket, " put it to her Ladyship to clear that up. Put it to her Ladyship, if you think it right, from Inspector Bucket of the Detective. You'll find, or I'm much mistaken, that the deceased Mr. Tulkinghorn had the intention of communicating the whole to you, as soon as he considered it ripe; and further, that he had given her Ladyship so to understand. Why, he might have been going to reveal it the very morning when I examined the body! You don't know what I'm going to say and do, five minutes from this present time, Sir Leicester Dedlock, Baronet; and supposing I was to be picked off now, you might wonder why I hadn't done it, don't you see? "

Sir Leicester seems to wake, though his eyes have been wide open; and he looks intently at Mr. Bucket, as Mr. Bucket refers to his watch.

" The party to be apprehended is now in this house," proceeds Mr. Bucket, putting up his watch with a steady hand, and with rising spirits, " and I'm about to take her into custody in your presence. Sir Leicester Dedlock, Baronet, don't you say a word, nor yet stir. There'll be no noise, and no disturbance at all. I'll come back in the course of the evening, if agreeable to you, and endeavor to meet your wishes respecting this unfortunate family matter, and the nobbiest way of keeping it quiet. Now, Sir Leicester Dedlock, Baronet, don't you be nervous on account of the apprehension at present coming off. You shall see the whole case clear, from first to last."

Mr. Bucket rings, goes to the door, briefly whispers Mercury, shuts the door, and stands behind it with his arms folded. After a suspense of a minute or two, the door slowly opens, and a Frenchwoman enters. Mademoiselle Hortense.

The moment she is in the room, Mr. Bucket claps the door to, and puts his back up against it. The suddenness of the noise occasions her to turn; and then, for the first time she sees Sir Leicester Dedlock in his chair.

"I ask you pardon," she mutters hurriedly. "They tell me there was no one here."

Her step towards the door brings her front to front with Mr. Bucket. Suddenly a spasm shoots across her face, and she turns deadly pale.

"This is my lodger, Sir Leicester Dedlock," says Mr. Bucket, nodding at her. "This foreign young woman has been my lodger for some weeks back."

"What do Sir Leicester care for that, you think, my angel?" returns Mademoiselle, in a jocular strain.

"Why, my angel," returns Mr. Bucket, "we shall see."

Mademoiselle Hortense eyes him with a scowl upon her tight face, which generally changes into a smile of scorn. "You are very mysterieuse. Are you drunk?"

"Tolerable sober, my angel," returns Mr. Bucket.

"I come from arriving at this so detestable house with your wife. Your wife have left me since some minutes. They tell me downstairs that your wife is here. I come here, and your wife is not here. What is the intention of this fool's play, say then?" Mademoiselle demands, with her arms composedly crossed, but with something in her dark cheek beating like a clock.

Mr. Bucket merely shakes the finger at her.

"Ah, my God, you are an unhappy idiot!" cries Mademoiselle, with a toss of her head and a laugh.—"Leave me to pass downstairs, great pig." With a stamp of her foot, and a menace.

"Now, Mademoiselle," says Mr. Bucket, in a cool determined way, "you go and sit down upon that sofy."

"I will not sit down upon nothing," she replies, with a shower of nods.

"Now, Mademoiselle," repeats Mr. Bucket, making no demonstration, except with the finger, "you sit down upon that sofy."

" Why ? "

" Because I take you into custody on the charge of murder, and you don't need to be told it. Now, I want to be polite to one of your sex and a foreigner, if I can. If I can't, I must be rough; and there's rougher ones outside. What I am to be depends on you. So I recommend you, as a friend, afore another half a blessed moment has passed over your head, to go and sit down upon the sofy."

Mademoiselle complies, saying in a concentrated voice, while that something in her cheek beats fast and hard, " You are a Devil."

" Now, you see," Mr. Bucket proceeds approvingly, " you're comfortable, and conducting yourself as I should expect a foreign young woman of your sense to do. So I'll give you a piece of advice, and it's this, Don't you talk too much. You're not expected to say anything here, and you can't keep too quiet a tongue in your head. In short, the less you Parlay, the better, you know." Mr. Bucket is very complacent over this French explanation.

Mademoiselle, with that tigerish expansion of the mouth, and her black eyes darting fire upon him, sits upright on the sofa in a rigid state, with her hands clenched—and her feet too, one might suppose—muttering, " O, you Bucket, you are a Devil ! "

" Now, Sir Leicester Dedlock, Baronet," says Mr. Bucket, and from this time forth the finger never rests, " this young woman, my lodger, was her Ladyship's maid at the time I have mentioned to you ; and this young woman, besides being extraordinary vehement and passionate against her Ladyship after being discharged——"

" Lie ! " cries Mademoiselle. " I discharged myself."

" Now, why don't you take my advice ? " returns Mr. Bucket, in an impressive, almost in an imploring tone. " I'm surprised at the indiscreetness you commit. You'll say something that'll be used against you, you know. You're sure to come to it. Never you mind what I say till it's given in evidence. It is not addressed to you."

" Discharge, too ! " cries Mademoiselle, furiously, " by

her Ladyship! Eh, my faith, a pretty Ladyship! Why, I r-r-r-ruin my character by remaining with a Ladyship so infame!"

"Upon my soul I wonder at you!" Mr. Bucket remonstrates. "I thought the French were a polite nation, I did, really. Yet to hear a female going on like that, before Sir Leicester Dedlock, Baronet!"

"He is a poor abused!" cries Mademoiselle. "I spit upon his house, upon his name, upon his imbecility," all of which she makes the carpet represent. "Oh, that he is a great man! O yes, superb! O Heaven! Bah!"

"Well, Sir Leicester Dedlock," proceeds Mr. Bucket, "this intemperate foreigner also angrily took it into her head that she established a claim upon Mr. Tulkinghorn, deceased, by attending on the occasion I told you of, at his chambers; though she was liberally paid for her time and trouble."

"Lie!" cries Mademoiselle. "I ref-use his money altogezzer."

("If you *will* Parlay, you know," says Mr. Bucket, parenthetically, "you must take the consequences.) Now, whether she became my lodger, Sir Leicester Dedlock, with any deliberate intention then of doing this deed and blinding me, I give no opinion on; but she lived in my house, in that capacity, at the time that she was hovering about the chambers of the deceased Mr. Tulkinghorn with a view to a wrangle, and likewise persecuting and half frightening the life out of an unfortunate stationer."

"Lie!" cries Mademioselle. "All lie!"

"The murder was committed, Sir Leicester Dedlock, Baronet, and you know under what circumstances. Now, I beg of you to follow me close with your attention for a minute or two. I was sent for, and the case was intrusted to me. I examined the place, and the body, and the papers, and everything. From information I received (from a clerk in the same house) I took George into custody, as having been seen hanging about there, on the night, and at very nigh the time, of the murder, also, as having been overheard in high words with the deceased on former occasions—even threatening him, as the witness made out. If you ask me, Sir Leicester Dedlock, whether from the first I believed George to be the murderer, I tell you candidly No; but he might be, notwithstanding; and there was enough against him to make it my duty to take him, and get him kept under remand. Now, observe!"

As Mr. Bucket bends forward in some excitement—for him—and inaugurates what he is going to say with one ghostly beat of his forefinger in the air, Mademoiselle Hortense fixes her black eyes upon him with a dark frown, and sets her dry lips closely and firmly together.

"I went home, Sir Leicester Dedlock, Baronet, at night, and found this young woman having supper with my wife, Mrs. Bucket. She had made a mighty show of being fond of Mrs. Bucket from her first offering herself as our lodger, but that night she made more than ever—in fact, overdid it. Likewise, she overdid her respect, and all that, for the lamented memory of the deceased Mr. Tulkinghorn. By the living Lord, it flashed upon me, as I sat opposite to her at the table and saw her with a knife in her hand, that she had done it!"

Mademoiselle is hardly audible, in straining through her teeth and lips the words "You are a Devil."

"Now where," pursues Mr. Bucket, "had she been on the night of the murder? She had been to the theayter. (She really was there, I have since found, both before the deed and after it.) I knew I had an artful customer to deal with, and that proof would be very difficult; and I laid a trap for her—such a trap as I never laid yet, and such a venture as I never made yet. I worked it out in my mind while I was talking to her at supper. When I went upstairs to bed, our house being small and this young woman's ears sharp, I stuffed the sheet into Mrs. Bucket's mouth that she shouldn't say a word of surprise, and told her all about it.—My dear, don't you give your mind to that again, or I shall link your feet together at the ankles." Mr. Bucket, breaking off has made a noiseless descent upon Mademoiselle, and laid his heavy hand upon her shoulder.

"What is the matter with you now?" she asked him.

"Don't you think any more," returns Mr. Bucket, with admonitory finger, "of throwing yourself out of window. That's what's the matter with me. Come! Just take my arm. You needn't get up; I'll sit down by you. Now take my arm, will you? I'm a married man, you know; you're acquainted with my wife. Just take my arm."

Vainly endeavoring to moisten those dry lips, with a painful sound, she struggles with herself and complies.

"Now we're all right again. Sir Leicester Dedlock, Baronet, this case could never have been the case it is, but for Mrs. Bucket, who is a woman in fifty thousand—in a hundred and fifty thousand! To throw this young woman off her guard, I have never set foot in our house since; though I've communicated with Mrs. Bucket, in the baker's loaves and in the milk, as often as required. My whispered words to Mrs. Bucket, when she had the sheet in her mouth, were, 'My dear, can you throw her off continually with natural accounts of my suspicions against George, and this, and that, and t'other? Can you do without rest, and keep watch upon her, night and day? Can you undertake to say, She shall do nothing without my knowledge, she shall be my prisoner without suspecting it, she shall no more escape from me than from death, and her life shall be my life, and her soul my soul, till I have got her, if she did this murder?' Mrs. Bucket says to me, as well as she could speak, on account of the sheet, 'Bucket, I can!' And she has acted up to it glorious!"

"Lies!" Mademoiselle interposes. "All lies, my friend!"

"Sir Leicester Dedlock, Baronet, how did my calculations come out under these circumstances? When I calculated that this impetuous young woman would overdo it in new directions, was I wrong or right? I was right. What does she try to do? Don't let it give you a turn? To throw the murder on her Ladyship?"

Sir Leicester rises from his chair, and staggers down again.

"And she got encouragement in it from hearing that I was always here, which was done a' purpose. Now, open that pocket-book of mine, Sir Leicester Dedlock, if I may take the liberty of throwing it towards you, and look at the letters sent to me, each with the two words, LADY DEDLOCK, in it. Open the one directed to yourself, which I stopped this very morning, and read the three words, LADY DEDLOCK, MURDERESS, in it. These letters have been falling about like a shower of lady-birds. What do you say now to Mrs. Bucket, from her spy-place, having seen them all written by this young woman? What do you say to Mrs. Bucket having, within this half-hour, secured the corresponding ink and paper, fellow half-sheets and what not? What do you say to Mrs. Bucket having watched the posting of 'em every one by this young woman, Sir Leicester Dedlock, Baronet?" Mr. Bucket asks, triumphant in his admiration of his lady's genius.

Two things are especially observable, as Mr. Bucket proceeds to a conclusion. First, that he seems imperceptibly to establish a dreadful right of property in Mademoiselle. Secondly, that the very atmosphere she breathes seems to narrow and contract about her, as if a close net, or a pall, were being drawn nearer and yet nearer around her breathless figure.

"There is no doubt that her Ladyship was on the spot at the eventful period," says Mr. Bucket; "and my foreign friend here saw her, I believe, from the upper part of the staircase. Her Ladyship and George and my foreign friend were all pretty close on one another's heels. But that don't signify any more, so I'll not go into it. I found the wadding of the pistol with which the deceased Mr. Tulkinghorn was shot. It was a bit of the printed description of your house at Chesney Wold. Not much in that, you'll say, Sir Leicester Dedlock, Baronet. No. But when my foreign friend here is so thoroughly off her guard as to think it a safe time to tear up the rest of that leaf, and when Mrs. Bucket puts the pieces together and finds the wadding wanting, it begins to look like Queer Street."

" These are very long lies," Mademoiselle interposes. " You prose great deal. Is it that you have almost all finished, or are you speaking always? "

" Sir Leicester Dedlock, Baronet," proceeds Mr. Bucket, who delights in a full title, and does violence to himself when he dispenses with any fragment of it, " the last point in the case which I am now going to mention, shows the necessity of patience in our business, and never doing a thing in a hurry. I watched this young woman yesterday, without her knowledge, when she was looking at the funeral, in company with my wife, who planned to take her there; and I had so much to convict her, and I saw such an expression in her face, and my mind so rose against her malice towards her Ladyship, and the time was altogether such a time for bringing down what you may call retribution upon her, that if I had been a younger hand with less experience, I should have taken her, certain. Equally, last night, when her Ladyship, as is so universally admired I am sure, come home, looking—why, Lord! a man might almost say like Venus rising from the ocean, it was so unpleasant and inconsistent to think of her being charged with a murder of which she was innocent, that I felt quite to want to put an end to this job. What should I have lost? Sir Leicester Dedlock, Baronet, I should have lost the weapon. My prisoner here proposed to Mrs. Bucket, after the departure of the funeral, that they should go, per bus, a little ways into the country, and take tea at a very decent house of entertainment. Now, near that house of entertainment there's a piece of water. At tea, my prisoner got up to fetch her pocket-handkercher from the bedroom where the bonnets was; she was rather a long time gone, and came back a little out of wind. As soon as they came home this was reported to me by Mrs. Bucket, along with her observations and suspicions. I had the piece of water dragged by moonlight, in presence of a couple of our men, and the pocket-pistol was brought up before it had been there a half a dozen hours. Now, my dear, put your arm a little further through mine, and hold it steady, and I shan't hurt you!"

In a trice Mr. Bucket snaps a handcuff on her wrist. "That's one," says Mr. Bucket. "Now the other, darling. Two, and all told!"

He rises; she rises too. "Where," she asks him, darkening her large eyes until their drooping lids almost conceal them—and yet they stare, "where is your false, your treacherous and cursed wife?"

"She's gone forard to the Police Office," returns Mr. Bucket. "You'll see her there, my dear."

"I would like to kiss her!" exclaims Mademoiselle Hortense, panting tigress-like.

"You'd bite her, I suspect," says Mr. Bucket.

"I would!" making her eyes very large. "I would love to tear her, limb from limb."

"Bless you, darling," says Mr. Bucket, with the greatest composure; "I am fully prepared to hear that. Your sex have such a surprising animosity against one another, when you do differ. You don't mind me half so much, do you?"

"No. Though you are a devil still."

"Angel and devil by turns, eh?" cries Mr. Bucket. "But I am in my regular employment, you must consider. Let me put your shawl tidy. I've been lady's maid to a good many before now. Anything wanting to the bonnet? There's a cab at the door."

Mademoiselle Hortense, casting an indignant eye at the glass, shakes herself perfectly neat in one shake, and looks, to do her justice, uncommonly genteel.

"Listen then, my angel," says she, after several sarcastic nods: "You are very spiritual. But can you restore him back to life?"

Mr. Bucket answers, "Not exactly."

"That is droll. Listen yet one time. You are very spiritual. Can you make an honorable lady of Her?"

"Don't be so malicious," says Mr. Bucket.

"Or a haughty gentleman of *Him?*" cries Mademoiselle,

referring to Sir Leicester with ineffable disdain. "Eh!
O then regard him! The poor infant! Ha! ha! ha!"

"Come, come, why, this is worse parlaying than the
other," says Mr. Bucket. "Come along!"

"You cannot do these things? Then you can do as you
please with me. It is but the death, it is all the same. Let
us go, my angel. Adieu you old man, gray. I pity you,
and I des-pise you!"

With these last words, she snaps her teeth together, as
if her mouth closed with a spring. It is impossible to
describe how Mr. Bucket gets her out, but he accomplishes
that feat in a manner so peculiar to himself; enfolding and
pervading her like a cloud, and hovering away with her
as if he were a homely Jupiter, and she the object of his
affections.

Sir Leicester, left alone, remains in the same attitude,
as though he were still listening, and his attention were still
occupied. At length he gazes round the empty room, and
finding it deserted, rises unsteadily to his feet, pushes back
his chair, and walks a few steps, supporting himself by the
table. Then he stops; and, with more of those inarticulate
sounds, lifts up his eyes and seems to stare at something.

Heaven knows what he sees. The green, green woods
of Chesney Wold, the noble house, the pictures of his forefathers, strangers defacing them, officers of police coarsely
handling his most precious heirlooms, thousands of fingers
pointing at him, thousands of faces sneering at him. But
if such shadows flit before him to his bewilderment, there
is one other shadow which he can name with something like
distinctness even yet, and to which alone he addresses his
tearing of his white hair, and his extended arms.

It is she, in association with whom, saving that she
has been for years a main fiber of the root of his dignity
and pride, he has never had a selfish thought. It is she
whom he has loved, admired, honored, and set up for the
world to respect. It is she, who, at the core of all the
constrained formalities and conventionalities of his life, has
been a stock of living tenderness and love, susceptible as

nothing else is of being struck with the agony he feels. He sees her, almost to the exclusion of himself; and cannot bear to look upon her cast down from the high place she has graced so well.

And, even to the point of his sinking on the ground oblivious of his suffering, he can yet pronounce her name with something like distinctness in the midst of those intrusive sounds, and in a tone of mourning and compassion rather than reproach.